DREAMGIRLS

A novelization by DENENE MILLNER
Based on the screenplay by BILL CONDON

HarperEntertainment
An Imprint of HarperCollins*Publishers*

This is a work of fiction. Names, characters, places, and incidents are products of the author's imagination or are used fictitiously and are not to be construed as real. Any resemblance to actual events, locales, organizations, or persons, living or dead, is entirely coincidental.

HARPERENTERTAINMENT
An Imprint of HarperCollins*Publishers*
10 East 53rd Street
New York, New York 10022-5299

ISBN-13: 978-0-06-123144-5
ISBN-10: 0-06-123144-4

First HarperEntertainment paperback printing: November 2006

Printed in the United States of America

Visit HarperEntertainment on the World Wide Web at www.harpercollins.com

10 9 8 7 6 5 4 3 2 1

For all the girls who've dared to dream, and all those after them who were smart enough to recognize that it's on the dreamgirls' wings that they soar.

ONE

"Effie, will you come on here?" Deena snapped over her shoulder as she raced toward the theatre, her left hand holding down the wig that, with every pronounced step, threatened to teeter off her head, her right clutching her mother's apricot church shoes. She'd snuck those shoes out of her mother's closet moments after May Jones left for her PTA meeting, and prayed the whole hour and a half while her mother was gone that she (a) would hurry back and be so dead tired from her long day teaching third grade and arguing with the parents of Spruce Street Elementary School that she'd go straight to sleep without making a big fuss over what time Deena turned the lights out, and (b) wouldn't come back in the house looking for those shoes. They were the perfect complement to the apricot gowns she and her best friends Effie and Lorrell sewed special for the Monday night R&B competition at the Detroit Theatre, and she simply would not be able to perform the steps with grace and distinction if she didn't have those shoes. The good news was that her mother was so beat that instead of turning on the light and tapping Deena's shoulder to let her know she was home, May simply stuck her head in Deena's room, then quietly shut the door, walked back into the living room, and tucked into the pull-out sofa, completely unaware that her child was stuffed under her bedspread in full clothes and makeup, waiting to sneak out into the darkness and toward her shot at stardom. The bad news? May came home much later than Deena planned and decided to unwind with a little reading, which meant that it was an incredibly long time before Deena could sneak out. And now the Dreamettes were almost an hour late for their slot in the competition.

"Look, I'm going as fast as I can, but it ain't easy getting all of this woman to run top speed in heels," Effie huffed, trailing way behind the much more agile Deena and Lorrell. Effie's brother, C.C., having had to stop and pick up the sheet music and makeup kit he'd dropped all across the sidewalk, was bringing up the rear. "Besides, we ain't missing our spot because I'm not running fast enough, Miss My Mama Got Home Late, so don't try to put this on me."

"Just come on," Deena huffed, picking up her pace.

Lorrell, who reached the theatre first, stopped dead in her tracks under the huge marquee, which had so many lights, it illuminated almost the entire length of the block. A smile slowly spread across her face as she read the words:

TONIGHT
JAMES THUNDER EARLY
PLUS LOCAL TALENT REVUE

The theatre, which in its heyday had been an opulent movie palace that showcased newsreels and silent films for white audiences, was a shell of its former self—the seats and carpet and the grand flowing red curtain long molded and dusty from years of abuse and neglect. But it came alive every Monday evening—the only night the cash-strapped owners allowed coloreds in the theatre's seats—when the local black radio station hosted its hugely popular Motor City Revue, which was attended by most anybody who had some dress clothes and the $2.50 to get through the door. Even R&B stars like James "Thunder" Early, a local boy gone big with a few soul hits rotating on black stations, knew that if they were touring in Detroit, they'd best talk their way onto the Monday night marquee if they'd wanted to really get some love in the Motor City.

Deena rushed past her and into the theatre's backstage alley, where contestants dressed in flashy tuxes and spectacular gowns dragged on cigarettes and drank from half-empty whiskey flasks, taking a break from the raucous show inside. She almost ran face-first into two well-heeled ladies who were rushing out the door, suitcases in hand, and in an apparent argument with a man who was begging them to stop and listen.

"Ladies, come on now, you can't leave. What about the show? What about Jimmy?" he asked, touching one of the women on the shoulder.

"Marty, you know I can talk," the woman said, snatching her shoulder away. "Now watch me walk."

"Joann, sugar, Jimmy was just bein' Jimmy. You know he's crazy 'bout you. Just crazy."

"Oh really? Well why don't you give the crazy man a message from me?" Joann said, stopping to face Marty. "Tell him I got his number. His phone number."

"Now baby—"

The woman cut him off. "At home. Where he lives. With *his wife*."

Joann's friend, who looked equally pissed, pushed past Deena, who'd stopped short when she saw the two beautiful women, exquisitely dressed in beaded gowns and jewels Deena had never seen, except in the occasional magazine she snuck and read in the library when she was supposed to be studying. Their beauty made Deena quite conscious of her bony, delicate frame (not to mention her raggedy homemade gown); and their voices, rich and smoky and loud, made her nearly shrink into the wall. How, she thought, would the Dreamettes ever be able to compete with those grown women?

"Come on, Joann. Our limousine is waiting," the woman said, jutting her chin out toward a junky taxicab that had pulled up in front of the theatre.

"Shit," Marty said, tossing a look at the crowd that had turned its attention to the drama before pushing past a slick-suited man who was, by then, holding the stage door open for him.

"Hey mister," the man said as Marty rushed by. "Can I interest you in the sound of tomorrow?"

Marty spit out his cigarette and went back inside the theatre without saying a word. Curtis quickly stopped the stage door with his foot, a move that snapped Deena out of the trance she'd fallen into as she followed the back-alley theatrics. "Oh my God, we're too late!" she yelled.

Deena looked at the man left standing in the alley, his face crumpled in dejection, and, reminded of her own dire circumstances, snapped herself out of her moment of fear. Deena decided they'd practiced too long, hoped for their big break too hard to turn around now, no matter how scared she was. Besides, Effie would kill her if she tried to turn her back on the stage now. Deena squared her shoulders and walked over to a man with a slick pompadour and a cheap suit, leaning up against the wall, a cigarette dangling from his lips. "Hey, you go on yet?" she asked hurriedly.

"About an hour ago," he said nonchalantly.

Deena rushed back to the front of the theatre and snatched Lorrell by her arm. "Come on, we have to get in there," she said, running toward the backstage door. "And where's Effie?"

Lorrell, moving in lockstep with Deena, looked back to see C.C. huffing right behind them. "C.C., go on back there and help your sister, now," she said, as the two of them burst through the door, knocking smack into Mr. Slick Suit.

"Oh, I'm sorry, mister," Deena said as Lorrell ran into her, almost making Deena and the man collide again. They could hear the raucous crowd clapping and cheering on Little Albert & the Tru-Tones, a group from the same projects as the Dreamettes. Deena, Lorrell, and Effie watched them perform that same song, "Goin' Downtown," in the courtyard practically every day after school while they, too, warmed up their voices and worked on their own dance steps. By the sound of the audience, all that practice was paying off.

"Taylor. Curtis Taylor, Jr.," the man said as an introduction, seemingly not fazed by the hapless girls. But Deena didn't really hear him; her attention had already moved on to Oak, the talent show's booker, who was rushing by with a clipboard in his hand. She stepped out in front of Oak and gave his chest a gentle push with her hand.

"Look, I know we're late, but my mama, she don't like me goin' out on weeknights, so I had to wait for her to go to bed—"

Oak impatiently cut her off. "Who are you?"

"Deena Jones," she said, wriggling out of her coat and forcing a thousand-watt smile to her face. "One of the Dreamettes."

The booker kept looking at his clipboard, barely paying attention to the words coming out of Deena's mouth. "You were supposed to go on second."

"I know," Deena stammered. "But my mother stayed out late at a PTA meeting. See she's a grade school teacher—"

"Tough luck, kid. Show's over," he said simply, turning to move on back to his business. But he was stopped in his tracks by Curtis, who put a firm hand on his shoulder and leaned into him. He towered over the officious man with the pencil moustache; his look was menacing, dark—almost sinister.

"Brother, let me lay somethin' down for you," he said quietly, leaning into Oak's ear, Oak's shoulder still in his firm grip. "I can tell you're a good man, so I don't want you comin' up weak here. Low-rating people—now that ain't what you got into this business for. Am I right? So what do you say we give these girls a break tonight?"

Curtis relaxed his grip and gave Oak's shoulder a friendly squeeze. Deena heard the music come to an end, punctuated by thunderous applause and the rumbling voice of the night's announcer. Oak looked at his shoulder and then back at Curtis, somewhat intimidated, definitely annoyed. "Okay," he said finally. "I'll put her on last. After Tiny Joe Dixon."

"Oh thank you!" Deena said excitedly, grabbing for Lorrell's hand. "Which one is Tiny?"

Oak motioned to a huge man—had to be at least six-three, 250-plus pounds. Muscles bulged out of the arms and shoulders of his ill-fitting suit jacket, over which he'd slung his guitar. He strutted past them as the M.C., Frank Evans, called out, "Ladies and gentlemen—Tiny Joe Dixoooooon!"

forcing Deena and Lorrell and practically everyone else in his path to shrink back against the wall to give him room.

"Uh-huh. Dressing room's that way," Oak said, jutting his chin toward a small holding area roped off from the rest of the backstage. It was filthy—dirty napkins and tissues and paper cups were strewn all over the worn-down carpet, ashtrays were filled to the brim with lipstick-stained cigarettes. A row of illuminated makeup mirrors hung precariously from the back wall, just beyond a few folding chairs.

Deena and Lorrell rushed over to the mirror in the dressing area and began to adjust their wigs, which they'd purchased just two days before with money they scraped up doing odd jobs and taking in laundry from white ladies too busy or too good to wash their own clothes. Neither of the girls could hardly contain herself when they squeezed into Lorrell's tiny bathroom to try on the dark brown bobs that shimmied and shook with every gyration and shoulder shake they made. "These wigs are going to put us on the map when we get to that talent show," Deena said, striking a pose.

C.C. rushed into the dressing area, the sound of Tiny Joe Dixon's guitar licks and "baby, baby" wails nearly drowning him out. "I got the music to the drummer," he screamed excitedly, dropping the makeup bag on the crowded counter.

"C.C., we're on next—where's Effie?" Deena rushed.

"I'm right here," Effie said, sauntering into the holding area, her distinctive black and white faux leopard-skin coat every bit as captivating as she. Out of breath, she leaned against the wall, untied her do rag, and adjusted the huge gaggle of synthetic hair that dwarfed her head. "God, I need to rest. Where's our dressing room?" she asked, crinkling her nose as she took in the dirty room.

"Effie, there's no time for that," Lorrell said, adjusting a safety pin in the front of her dress, a move that made her cleavage more pronounced. "We go on in two minutes!"

Effie snapped to attention. "What?"

"Come on—let's warm up," Deena said, rushing over to Lorrell and counting off the beat. Lorrell moved lockstep with her, swaying as they harmonized: *"Move, move/Move right out of my life . . ."*

They stopped singing when they got a gander of the Stepp Sisters, who, coming off a successful stage performance, were slinking past with all kinds of attitude. They stopped in their tracks, though, when they saw the Dreamettes. There were enough audible gasps to change the air pressure in the backstage area. "Oh no—they're wearing our wigs!" Deena exclaimed.

"We're ruined unless we can find new wigs," Lorrell said. "Everyone's going to think we stole our look from them!"

"Why do we need wigs in the first place?" asked Effie, clearly annoyed.

"Because we need a look," Deena huffed as she turned back toward the mirror and snatched her wig around. Honestly, she just didn't get why Effie didn't understand that a group needed to be cohesive—have some kind of uniformity about it. It wasn't, after all, Effie and the Dreamettes, even if her brother wrote all the songs and she did sing all the leads. Presentation was what was going to make the Dreamettes a group to remember, Deena was constantly reminding Effie. "Please," Effie would always respond when they'd get into their "star" arguments, which usually occurred when they'd gather around Effie's TV set to watch *American Bandstand*. "They may think they look cute in those dresses, looking like a set of triplets. But ain't no way in hell you are ever going to look like me, and I sure as hell ain't gonna look like you any time soon," she'd laugh.

Deena stood back from the mirror and admired herself as she slicked down the hair, which was now flowing forward in an impossibly awkward angle—scooped in the back, longer in the front. "I got it—turn the wigs around!"

"What?" Lorrell said, staring at Deena.

"Turn the wigs around!"

The three crowded into the mirror, adjusting their hair and tucking bobby pins across their scalps to hold their new 'dos in place.

"Oh, Deena, it's so . . . different," Lorrell said, scrunching her eyes in hopes that the new hairstyle would look a little better than it actually did.

"It's sophisticated-looking. Come on!" Deena said, heading for the stage.

Effie, who was always really particular about the way she looked—especially next to her group mates—lingered to check herself out. She was not pleased. "Front ways or back ways, store-bought hair ain't natural. And what about these dresses? I mean, this dress does nothin' for my body."

Lorrell stopped, turned back, and rolled her eyes at Effie. "You got the same wig I got?"

"Yeah," Effie said, still fussing in the mirror.

"You got the same dress I got?"

"Yeah," Effie said, turning around to look Lorrell in the eye.

"Then shut up," Lorrell said, and walked away.

Effie turned her wig back around, and was fussing with it some more when Curtis stepped in behind her. "Say, miss, I think you look just great."

Effie gave a coquettish grin—a look that said,

Of course. And then she floated off after Deena and Lorrell, who had rushed into the wings to join the M.C.

"What's the name of your group again?" the M.C. asked.

"The Dreamettes," Deena said, leaning into him and yelling into his ear so he could hear her over Tiny Joe Dixon's wailing.

The M.C. thanked her by pinching Deena on her behind, a move that made Deena gasp out loud, and caught the attention of Effie, who saw the aging, greasy man touch her friend's ass. She moved in close and tapped on his shoulder; when he turned around, his eyes trailed from Effie's large, curvaceous bosom up to her fiery eyes. She stared him down like the bell was about to sound in the first round of a heavyweight fight. The M.C. backed away and rushed onto the stage as Tiny Joe walked off.

"And now, please welcome our final act, the courageous, the curvaceous . . . Creamettes!"

"It's the Dreamettes! The Dreamettes!" Deena screamed as she and Lorrell ran onstage and took their positions behind Effie. The band started up, and the heavy curtains squeaked their way to their corners, revealing huge, nearly blinding floodlights and dark silhouettes of what seemed to be hundreds of bodies, all waiting for the Dreamettes to sing their first notes. Lorrell stood frozen, unsure whether to sway in time with Deena or exit stage left, where she'd surely lose all hope of being a professional singer, but at least find a nice, quiet place to bury her head and hide from the rush of bodies and lights and high expectations. Deena, who wasn't much less frightened by the spectacle but had enough control over her nerves to sway to the music, took hold of Lorrell's hand and got her to move just a little bit as the music intro played on. Effie, standing center stage and completely clueless to her group mates' stage fright, felt the bass in the pit of her stomach and wiggled her body to the beat, taking in every ounce of the energy the musicians put into C.C.'s music, even if the crowd didn't seem at all moved. Then she began to blow; her voice was electrifying. *"You better move,"* she boomed into the mic as Deena and Lorrell harmonized, *"Move!"*

C.C. was watching from the wings, mimicking the steps he'd designed for them. Next to him was Curtis, who, intrigued, caught Effie's eye as she twirled. Effie put a little extra swing in her hip for the handsome gentleman who'd just paid her a compliment with more than just words.

Deena didn't notice all of that; instead, she was focused on the judges, one of whom was shaking his head, seemingly unimpressed by their unpolished, raw stage routine. Just then, Effie let loose, her voice soaring to the rafters—so distinct and powerful, even the unimpressed judge looked up, blown away.

By the time Effie sang her last, triumphant note, the audience was on its feet, roaring for more. Deena and Lorrell hugged each other and jumped up and down as Effie took her curtsies, as if she'd just performed for the queen herself.

"Come on!" the M.C. said, rushing back out onto the stage as the girls took their bows. "You can do better for the delectable, the delicious, the defiant Dreamettes!"

The crowd was still roaring for the girls as they and all the other contestants waited in the wings while the judges sorted through who should win. As they tallied their scorecards, Curtis made his way out to the theatre lobby, and tapped on the shoulder of the M.C., who'd gone out front for a cigarette break. Curtis held up five ten-dollar bills. "Five dimes says the Dreamettes don't win," he said.

The M.C. snatched the money from Curtis's hand. "You got it," he smiled. "They weren't gonna win anyway," he added before stomping on his cigarette and heading back inside.

Moments later, the contestants were all ushered back onstage; the girls, who were standing dead center stage, were supremely confident they were about to take home the prize.

"Now remember, the winner of this year's contest gets a week's paid engagement right here at the Detroit Theatre," the M.C. said, as the booker handed him the results. "And that very lucky, very talented Star of Tomorrow is . . ." a drum roll accompanied his next words. "Tiny Joe Dixon!"

Tiny Joe joined the M.C. on the lip of the stage as the house curtain lowered on the losers, and the theatrical lights faded—but there was light enough to see the pain of rejection and humiliation in each of the girls' eyes. "Does this mean we're not gonna be famous now?" Lorrell said, her eyes tearing up.

"Well, not tonight," Effie said, dejected. "Come on, let's go home."

C.C. handed Lorrell and Effie their coats, but Deena remained center stage—her anger palpable. "Why?" she demanded.

"Because I'm tired and I have to get up early for work, that's why we're leaving."

"No, I mean—what's the point? Lorrell, how old were we when we first started singing together?" Deena demanded.

"Twelve," Lorrell said.

"C.C., how many dances you dreamed up for

us? How many songs you got written down there in your notebook?" Deena asked, turning to C.C.

"I don't know—maybe a hundred," he said.

"And Effie. Effie, you ever met anyone who can sing as crazy as you?"

"No," Effie said confidently.

"And still we're getting nowhere. So I'm asking you—what is the point?"

Just then, Curtis stepped into view, followed by Jimmy Early's roadies, who were rolling in a baby grand piano. "The point is, you don't need an amateur contest—there ain't nothing amateur about you. What you need is a break, and I'm here to give it to you," he said to the women. "Thirty bucks each to sing behind Jimmy Early tonight."

"Jimmy Early!" Lorrell swooned, jumping up and down and clutching Deena.

"And a guaranteed ten-week engagement on the road, starting tomorrow morning, at four hundred dollars a week!" Curtis continued, playing off the excitement.

"Oh my," Deena gasped. "Four hundred? You swear?"

"If I'm lying, I'm dying. And Mr. Early's agreed to hire my aunt Ethel to watch out for you girls while you're away from home."

"Oh, Mama's gonna like that!" Deena said.

"Effie, can you believe it? We're gonna sing behind Jimmy Early!"

"I don't do backup," Effie said, as she moved toward Curtis, put her hand on her hip, and shifted one foot forward—a stance that put her so squarely close to his face, she could smell the peppermint on his breath.

"Come on, Effie. All we have to do is a few oohs and aahs," Deena said excitedly.

"I don't do oohs and aahs," Effie said simply.

"Now you look, Effie," Lorrell said, moving closer to Effie and raising her pointer finger. "This could be our big break."

"Singing backup is a trap. I'm sorry, mister, but we cannot accept your offer," Effie said simply.

Deena and Lorrell fell silent, unsure of what to say next. Curtis, recognizing which woman he had to win over, moved in closer to Effie. "Look, I know you're good and so do you. You're talented, and what's more, you are a stone-cold fox, baby." He smiled, his eyes running over her body.

Effie's stance softened just a little. Did he just call her a fox? She shifted from one foot to the other, and slightly poked out her chest. Yes, he was flirting with her—this handsome man with the slick hair and even slicker talk. She admitted to herself that even though she wouldn't normally be inclined to take sweet talk from strangers, this fellow was offering a real paying gig *and* calling her foxy. She smiled with her eyes, but kept her mouth shut to hear what else he had to say.

"But that ain't enough," Curtis continued. "A girl like you could get hurt without someone there to protect you."

Effie's resolve started to wilt. She looked down and then over at her girls, who were still giving her their pleading eyes. Until now, she was the one doing most of the work—getting them gigs, chasing down their money, getting up more cash to keep their costumes fresh. Perhaps, she thought, a little help wouldn't be the death of her.

"I could do it for you, baby, but you've got to trust me," Curtis continued. "Believe me, I won't disappoint you."

"Come on, Effie, what do you say?" Deena asked.

"Well, mister . . ."

"Curtis Taylor, Jr."

"Curtis Taylor, Jr.—our manager—says we're singing behind Jimmy Early tonight!" Effie yelled.

Deena and Lorrell lunged toward Effie, knocking Curtis out of the way as they hugged and kissed their friend. "Oh, I love you, Effie!"

"Lord, this business sure does have its ups and downs," Lorrell said, grinning.

"Ladies, stay right here—I'll be right back. Let me go handle your business," Curtis said, backing out of the holding area and running down the hall. Effie tilted her head and watched him as he took off. Yeah, he would do just fine, she figured. Just fine.

James "Thunder" Early hardly let his manager, Marty, walk into the room before he jumped out of his seat and lit into him. "Marty, I said no mayonnaise! How many times do I got to tell you, no mayonnaise on the chicken sandwich?"

"We got bigger problems, baby. I warned you to lay off the women you work with. There are plenty of other ladies out there . . ."

"There sure are, but who's got the time to go out looking?" Jimmy said, grinning as he adjusted his sparkling red smoking jacket and sat back down to his dressing room table. He picked up the bread off his sandwich and used an old napkin to wipe off the mayo as he stared into the mirror, first at one side of his shiny, slicked-back hair, then at the other. "I'm always working!" The keyboardist and four trumpet players, who were over in the corner carrying on a furious game of craps, punctuated Jimmy's joke with a chorus of laughter.

"Yeah, 'cause Marty always keeps you working—c'mon." Marty beamed.

Just then, the lights in the theatre blinked on and off, signaling the audience that the show was about to start again. "Are you ready for Jimmy Early?" the M.C. screamed into the mic. The audience sent up a thunderous roar and started stomping so hard, the floorboards of the old theatre trembled. Jimmy stood up, adjusted his jacket again, and leaned into the mirror. He licked his finger and used his spit to smooth down his moustache, and then ran his hands across his hair.

"Check it out, Marty's worked it out for you," Marty said, his voice barely audible over the theatre noise. "I got this dynamite group of girls willing to fill in tonight."

"Great," Jimmy said, hardly paying attention.

"Thing is, there's three of them."

"I only need two," Jimmy quickly shot back. "That's more than enough to handle. You add three broads to my mix and the next thing you know, I'm spending all my time trying to keep them in line—won't be no shine for James 'Thunder' Early."

"But—"

"But, hell, Marty. I just need two."

Marty shrugged his shoulders, nodded his head, and checked his watch. "All right then, two. We should start heading out."

Marty and Jimmy were making their way out

to the stage, the keyboardist and trumpet players in tow, when Marty ran into Curtis, who'd been waiting anxiously outside the dressing room door, excitedly pacing back and forth. Curtis knew that if he could pull this off, he'd be well on his way to living out his dream of becoming a manager for crossover artists, a dream he'd had since the day he snuck into a juke joint in his father's rural Mississippi hometown and saw Lady Day fingering a gardenia in her hair as she creaked her way through "Good Morning, Heartache." As magnificent as Lady Day was, Curtis couldn't help but think what a waste it was that someone like Billie Holiday, with such a voice worthy of the angels, had to resort to singing in dirty watering holes south of nowhere, probably for little money, certainly for little accolade—even recognition. The world deserved to hear Billie, and she deserved that audience, no matter that she was colored—no matter the color of the audience. This much Curtis knew already. He was twelve.

Just a few years later, he'd dabbled a little bit in writing his own songs, trying, albeit unsuccessfully, to get them in the hands of established recording artists, and later, amateurs looking for some material that could stand out in local talent shows. He even married himself one of those amateurs, the daughter of a local car dealer who styled herself after Bessie Smith. Curtis loved her, which was the only reason he put his music ambitions on hold; she wanted him to help her daddy run his used Cadillac dealership, and he obliged, with a promise from the family that he could hone his business skills there, and eventually take over the family company. But Curtis never let go of his love of music; he relentlessly studied the industry in his spare time—drowning himself in the minutiae reported in *Billboard,* charting the success of the hottest groups, even dabbling in songwriting. When his father-in-law died, he willed Curtis the company (by then, his daughter was much more interested in chasing cocaine than she was car customers), and Curtis promptly began siphoning dealership profits to finance his foray into artist management. All he needed was a tiny opening to get his shot.

Curtis snapped to attention when he saw Jimmy. "Everything all set?" he asked anxiously.

"Yeah, Jimmy's down with the two girls," Marty said, pushing past him to follow behind his client.

Curtis looked down, trying to reconcile what he'd just heard. Two? "Aw hell," he muttered, before taking off to catch up with the star and his manager.

"Wait a minute, man," he called out, suddenly emboldened. "This is a group. It's three or nothing."

"What's happening, Marty?" Jimmy asked, annoyed. He stopped in his tracks.

"My clients always work together," Curtis said, walking decidedly slower to calm his nerves and appear more levelheaded. He squared his shoulders and looked Jimmy in the eye.

"Hey, I know you," Jimmy said, squinting to get a better look at Curtis. "Didn't you sell me my Cadillac?"

"Well . . . yeah," Curtis said weakly, not sure if he should be concerned about the connection. It wouldn't be the first time a former customer crawled in his ass the moment one of his cars started showing its wear. He stood his ground. "Yes. In addition to my management company, I own a car dealership down on Woodward Avenue."

Jimmy delivered a slick smile. He knew bull when he heard it. "Well, my kitty needs a tune-up, baby. And Jimmy only works with two."

"Sorry, brother. It's two or nothing," Marty chimed in, taking Jimmy's arm to lead him to the platform that would deliver Jimmy to the stage.

"Then it's nothing," Curtis said firmly as he watched them walk away.

Jimmy shrugged and stepped onto the platform. He steeled himself as Marty pressed the button that made the platform rise. He was shaking his shoulders and neck like a prize boxer just before the big fight when he caught an image of three sets of shapely legs on the stage. His eyes followed one set up the thigh, past the hips, and then up to the woman's breasts and finally her face as she and the other two girls stood there, giggling and excited to greet him. A wide grin spread across Jimmy's face when his eyes met Lorrell's. Lorrell's jaw dropped; clearly star-struck, she'd never met a kinda-sorta star before, much less someone whose music she actually heard on the radio. James "Thunder" Early was from the streets of Detroit, and so there weren't too many teens from the Motor City who didn't know who he was or who hadn't seen him in concerts around town. His stage show was electrifying; while his horns chewed on the music, Jimmy would shout and flip and stretch across the stage in an unseemly fit of acrobatics that made him one of the most exciting R&B performers in the business. Everybody tried to copy his style, but couldn't nobody move their hips, belt out a brassy tune, and funk up an overcrowded concert hall like Jimmy, who earned his nickname one hundred times over. Rumor had it that he had a fleet of fancy cars, a wife he kept dripping in diamonds, and a house in the hills, over where the white folks had them great big ol' houses and lawns that yawned on for acres.

Smitten that Jimmy was even paying her any mind, Lorrell waved, giggled some more, and then averted her eyes in Deena's direction. Deena, too, was excited, but Effie, ever the rock, was cool.

"Well, it's fine, Marty," Jimmy called back down the platform as he walked toward the girls, his arms outstretched to embrace the Dreamettes. "Three's gonna be just fine." Then, to the ladies, he said: "Ladies, you are saving Jimmy's life! I needed your help and I'm at your feet, thanking you!" He kneeled in front of Lorrell in gratitude, making her break into another fit of giggles. "Do you understand what I'm saying? I am thanking you. I will do anything for you. Anything. Now what can I do for you, baby?" he asked, taking her hand into his.

"Well, Mr. Early . . . You could teach us the song," Lorrell said timidly, her voice barely audible over the audience, which, by then, was screaming "Thunder! Thunder! Thunder!" after having grown impatient waiting for the curtain to open.

Jimmy jumped up and played a few chords on

the baby grand—the tinkling made the audience roar—and got to singing: *"Thirteen years of solid gold platters/Rising costs and cocktail chatter/Fat dee-jays, stereophonic sound/Oh baby!/The game of hits goes round and around."*

Jimmy got up from the grand when the key-boardist slid onto the bench, and walked over to Lorrell, crooning in her ear. *"But you can fake your way to the top/Round and around,"* he sang. "Try that part right there, baby."

Lorrell, nervous, sang the words, *"Round and around."*

"Fake your way to the top!" Jimmy said, this time with even more emphasis.

Deena chimed in, *"Round and around,"* her sweet voice making Jimmy smile.

"Yeah, you fell right in there, didn't you sweet-heart," he said, turning to her and swaying with her body. *"You can fake your way to the top,"* he sang some more.

"Round and around!" Effie boomed, her smoky, soulful voice bringing such force to the words that Jimmy jumped back.

"Shit, I knew you'd have it!" he laughed. *"But it's always real, so real,"* he sang.

"Always so real," the Dreamettes sang in unison, swaying to Jimmy's finger snaps and the pound-ing of the piano.

"Yeah," he said, giving the girls another once-over. "Yeah, three will do just fine."

"Y'all ready?" the M.C. asked as he rushed onto the stage.

"We ready," Jimmy said, taking his place.

The curtains opened, and Jimmy slid across the wood floor on his knees, screaming all the way to the middle of the stage, sending the crowd into an uncontrollable frenzy. Jimmy hopped up and executed a dazzling turn, whirling across the stage as a backdrop of trumpet players gyrated behind him, pulsating to their vocalist's frenetic rhythm. Jimmy continued to whirl and skip and jump, perspiration flying off his face as he poured every ounce of his soul into the microphone.

I know what's happenin'/I've been around
Faking my way/Through every town
I make my living/Off of my sound
And the game of hits/It goes around and around
And around and around/And around

The Dreamettes were all at once excited, frightened, and frazzled—they struggled to keep up with Jimmy and the band. Lorrell kept falling off beat, and Deena missed at least three of her cues as she rocked her hips and sang backup harmo-

nies, mesmerized by both Jimmy and espe
the way the crowd received him. Effie did her bes
to reel the girls in, calm their nerves, but it was no
use. They just couldn't compete with the master.
But they sure were going to learn.

TWO

You would have thought that C.C. was Effie's personal valet. There she was, alternately preening in the mirror and ordering her little brother to "put the makeup kit by the door so we don't forget it," and "fold my slip right so it doesn't get too many wrinkles, now!" and "quit fussing with my gowns and get them downstairs before Jimmy get here, C.C.!" And there he was, dutifully carrying out her wishes without so much as a mumble against Effie. That's the way it always was between them—Effie White would demand, Clarence Conrad White would appease. To outsiders, Effie appeared very much the bully, her brother a weakling who couldn't stand up for himself. But really, C.C. just looked up to his sister, whom he'd lovingly admired not just because she was the elder, and therefore automatically commanded his respect, but because he sincerely thought Effie was one of the most talented singers he'd ever heard, and his sister made him believe with every note she sang that he was the most talented undiscovered songwriter in Detroit. Their mutual admiration for each other, for sure, was very sincere—had been from the time Effie and C.C. would talk their pastor, the Reverend Goode Wright, into letting them stick around after Saturday choir practice and bang around on the piano. C.C., a self-taught musician who could play most any song by ear at the tender age of six, would make up little ditties, and Effie, who was three years his senior, would sing the words he gave her. By the time he was eleven, C.C. was the musical director of the Beulah Land Missionary Baptist Church's children's choir, and Effie? Well, she was his lead soloist.

Music, you see, was their glue. And no amount of divadom, sibling shenanigans, or treachery from outside forces could ever shake that bond.

"Lord have mercy, Effie, the bus is gonna be here any minute, girl," Lorrell yelled up to the open window of the White apartment as she impatiently waited with a small suitcase and raggedy garment bag out front, where Effie's father, Ronald, was standing at the ready to give the girls a proper send-off. Deena, who was holed up in the entryway of Effie's building after having just left on her mother's pillow a note about how she was sorry her mother didn't see the vision for her dream, but she was off to make it in show business, smushed her fingers to her lips, imploring Lorrell to quiet down, lest her mother wake up and catch her sneaking off with Jimmy, whom her mom called "Satan himself."

Ronald laughed as he pulled his hat down around his ears, a weak barrier against the morning chill. "She'll be down in a minute, darlin', don't you worry." Ronald chuckled. "Effie ain't gonna miss her chance to shine."

Lorrell sucked her teeth. "Effie ain't never missed her chance to shine, but she been known to miss a bus or two," she said, still looking at the window as if to will her best friend down. Lorrell, of all people, knew the difficulties of getting Effie White to respect schedules. They had, after all, been tight since Effie went into the fifth grade, when Lorrell, her three brothers, and their single mom moved into Building D of the broken-down project complex—the unfortunate consequence of her parents' nasty split. Lorrell had met Effie at the bus stop on her first day at her new school, singing a boisterous rendition of "Summertime." Lorrell, never one to shy away from capturing a little spotlight of her own, hummed the harmony, and before the bus could pull into the school parking lot, the two, with C.C. tapping out the beat on his weekly reader, had hammered out a duet so fierce, even the bus driver had to turn around and give them their due. Anxious to become professional singers, the two spent all of junior high singing in the school bathroom and dominating the school talent shows, and most of high school searching for a third singer to round out their trio after a local club owner told them they'd have a better shot getting into his popular talent show if Effie had more than one backup singer. Less than a week after that suggestion, Lorrell introduced Effie to Deena, the quiet, shy, doe-eyed daughter of her brother's third grade teacher. No one—not C.C., not Lorrell, not Deena; no one—was ever mistaken about who was the lead singer. And Effie milked her quasi project fame for all it was worth—staying out late, running boys, partying, and being as absolutely loud and fabulous as she could possibly be.

"Why you out here yelling up to my window like you in the projects?" Effie huffed as she walked out the heavy metal doors, C.C.—carrying a large suitcase, two paper bags, a makeup kit, and a garment bag—in tow.

"Uh, we are in the projects, darling," Lorrell said.

"Not for long," Effie said, pushing her chin toward the street, up which was riding a bright red, green, and silver bus with "James 'Thunder' Early" scrawled across the side. Deena, Lorrell, Effie, and C.C. all scrambled, suitcases and bags flying every which way as they excitedly headed toward the curb where the bus was pulling up.

"Just make me proud," C.C. called out, practically chasing the bus as it pulled off. With her hands pressed against the window, Effie mouthed her promise: *I will.*

But it wasn't long before she and the girls figured out just how hard it was to be proud on the chitlin' circuit. Wasn't a thing cute about traveling dirt roads all night to get to the next theatre, only to have owners dismiss their celebrity and treat them like all the other colored gals who walked through their doors. Most times they had to huddle in trashy, smoke-filled "coloreds only" rooms, waiting their turn to take the stage. It didn't really seem to matter to anyone else that they were Jimmy's backup singers—shoot, even Jimmy had to constantly sic Marty on the club owners' behinds to get him—the star—basic amenities, like a free drink or two, a hot plate of food from the kitchen, a place for him and the band to sit down for a spell while they got ready for the show. Sometimes, even his pay. It was, in a word, humiliating—waiting for one-trick ponies to grind their way through an evening's worth of mediocre performances before they could get on the stage and show everyone how it was done. One night in Chicago, Jimmy and the girls even had to sidestep dog poop on the stage after a dancer performed a lame two-step with his "dancing" pooch.

And Lord, if there was some little wannabe girl group hanging in the wings, trying to get noticed by somebody? Well, anyone could see that no matter how wide Lorrell had Jimmy's nose open, didn't none of the girls the Dreamettes ran into behind stage have a problem rounding up a little attention for themselves in hopes of getting on James "Thunder" Early's bus.

Still, the moment Jimmy spun his burly body onto those stages, the girls knew they were witnessing something otherworldly. All Jimmy had to do was bend his muscular legs, thrust his pelvis, cock his head, and let out a "Heeeeeeeeey," and the entire room would erupt into a roar of shouting and clapping and stomping and gyrating—like the Holy Spirit himself was moving through the crowd. Except wasn't nothing Saturday-night revival about Jimmy's performance. No, wasn't nothing holy about what Jimmy was stirring up.

"A man gets lonely," Jimmy wailed on one particular night at the Washington, D.C. theatre, Effie,

Lorrell, and Deena sweating behind him, laying down their *"do, do, do, dos"* in synch with their swaying, their arms flailing like Jimmy's energy was flowing through their bodies. By then, they'd watched his show at least ten times and rehearsed it a dozen more, and with each performance, they drank Jimmy in, watched him work the room, listened to his inflections, drooled over his timing and how he used it to wring out every ounce of emotion there was to be had from his panting audience. Effie and Deena were good at treating his performance like a good meal—they'd chew and swallow, and push themselves from the table. But Lorrell—well, she loved her Jimmy, and so she sucked on his performance like a fat man does a neckbone, swaying her hips a little extra hard so Jimmy would notice, and singing *"So he won't be alone"* right into Jimmy's eyes. Much to her surprise, she even found herself getting a little jealous when Jimmy launched into his signature flirt session with one of the fans in the Washington, D.C. theatre audience.

"Time to bring up the lights," Jimmy said as the keyboardist signaled the trumpet section and drummer to break the song down. Jimmy walked over to the lip of the stage, put his hands over his eyebrows, squinted, and looked out over the pulsating crowd. "Yeah, let's see which one of these ladies is goin' home with Jimmy tonight," he said, pushing the words out like a Baptist preacher. "Got a nice warm bed waitin' on you. C'mon now, who wants to sit on Daddy's lap?"

The women in the audience rushed the stage, held back by a couple of local policemen, who were really just Jimmy's roadies, dressed up in dime-store costumes and thrown a couple of extra bones for helping out on stage. Jimmy spotted a light-skinned beauty with long, shiny black hair and ordered "the police" to help her make her way to him. "Is your man here," he cooed to the woman as she giggled and moved in close to Jimmy's body. "What? He's in the bathroom? Hey, someone go out there and lock the bathroom." Then, Jimmy put the moves on his "fan." Lorrell knew the deal—the "girlfriend" was really the drummer's sister. But still, she didn't like the way she was looking at Jimmy, and she'd seen her pushing her way onto Jimmy's side of the bus when she thought nobody was paying her any mind.

The audience, electrified, cheered as Jimmy made his way back to center stage and beckoned the Dreamettes, who moved in a line toward him. *"Makes me feel so real,"* he sang, the music rising in a crescendo as he stepped back to the mike.

"Feel so real," Deena sang first into Jimmy's microphone, echoed by Effie. But when he got

to Lorrell, she locked her eyes with his, and let her hands linger on his as he handed her the microphone. *"Yeah it feels so real,"* she sang seductively.

It was that night that Lorrell decided she needed to get to "Harlem," the back of the bus where Curtis's aunt Ethel, the tour chaperone, cordoned off the boys. The girls? They were in "Hollywood," clean on the other side of the bus, and Aunt Ethel made it clear to the guys in the band, the roadies, and especially Jimmy that they "weren't welcome in Hollywood." Lorrell waited until Aunt Ethel was snoring hard enough to suck the upholstery off the seat before she checked her lipstick in her compact, and then climbed over the old woman's orthopedic shoes and made her way to the back of the bus. She patted her hair as she walked, and put on a huge grin when she saw Jimmy watching her bounce up to him. She twirled down into the empty space next to him. Without saying a word, he passed her his flask.

"Oh Mr. Early, I don't believe all of this can be happening to me," she said, smiling so hard she was practically showing back teeth.

"Miracles happen all the time in the world of R&B, baby." He smiled.

"What's R&B mean?"

Jimmy leaned in so close, there was hardly an

inch between their lips. "Rough and black," he practically whispered.

"Oh, Mr. Early, you're so crazy." She giggled, taken aback by his suggestion enough to scoot away from him, if only a little.

"Jimmy, baby. Call me Jimmy."

"Oh . . . Mr. Jimmy, you so crazy," she said, smiling harder as Jimmy slid closer and snuggled against her breast.

Though she was busy playing poker with Marty and one of the trumpet players, Effie was taking it all in. She tried to toss a look at Deena, but Deena was in her own cushioned world—a row that, with satiny pillows and a plush comforter, she managed to turn into a fluffy suite. Deena had gotten a little extra with her four-hundred-dollar checks—was always blowing off group dinners and after-rehearsal bonding sessions to rush off to spend her cash in some little "boutique" that didn't want her black behind up in it, or to play in her makeup and wigs, or just to go off by herself and sit like she wasn't part of the group. If Effie didn't know her any better, she would have thought Deena was trying to act like she was better than somebody. This, of course, wouldn't have been new, though, particularly since the girl's mother made her believe her little teacher's check made the two of them upper middle class. Can you imagine? Rich in the projects. Wasn't no telling how big Deena's head was going to swell off all of this. Effie rolled her eyes, shook her head, and turned back to her hand, but she tuned out her loud-talking card partners to listen in on Jimmy and Lorrell.

"You sure feel nice." Lorrell giggled, and then stopped almost as quickly as she started. She cleared her throat. "I mean, it feels funny. You're married, aren't you?"

Jimmy, who'd wed his high school sweetheart before the two of them turned seventeen and years before he'd struck it big with his hit single, shrugged off her question with a grin. "Yeah baby," Jimmy answered matter-of-factly. "Everybody knows Jimmy's married."

A frown quickly replaced Lorrell's smile. "Then you get your married hands off," she said, pulling free of Jimmy. He sat up to watch her walk away. "Um, um, um," he said, shifting his body to settle back into his nap. His eyes met Effie's.

Jimmy let out another little laugh and closed his eyes.

Deena and Effie huddled together at a corner table in the "Blue Bleu" club, an after-hours lounge they, Jimmy, and his entourage went to get a bite to eat after the concert. The girls tried to block out the blare of Jimmy's band jamming up on stage, but there was really not much use. They'd finally made it through the last set on their tour, and despite the fact that they were returning to the same desperate living situation that comes from being a resident of the poorest projects in the poorest part of Detroit, Jimmy, the Dreamettes, and their band were all looking forward to laying their heads down on their own mattresses—even if Jimmy's tour finale to his hometown crowd was less than triumphant.

Effie kicked off her shoes and propped them up on a freshly wiped chair she pulled down from the table next to the one where she and Deena were sitting, and looked around the supper club, quite the fancy word for such a small, ratty old bar that specialized in hard liquor and hot plates of fried chicken, corned beef hash, and hog maws. There wasn't much to the "Blue Bleu"; it was just a little hole in the wall that had long been a local nightspot favorite—the rickety chairs and peeling paint and chipped plates certainly attested to that. Colored folks made a point of wearing the tiny club out, and Ruby Mills, the club's owner, wasn't one to concern herself with candlelight and expensive silverware and waiters dressed to the nines. Indeed, the only thing that mattered to the patrons was the wooden dance floor and show time, or at least that's what Ruby'd say to justify spending her profits on everything but fixing the place up. Effie knew all this because she once served drinks there, hoping that her service would afford her a better shot at getting a stage gig there. Alas, that didn't quite work out; she got fired before anyone even knew she could blow—showed up late one too many times for Ruby's taste. Effie did quite enjoy walking into the club with Jimmy and his crew, though, her way of rubbing in to her former boss that she didn't need Ruby to make it big. Effie tossed a halfhearted wave at one of the few wait staff nearby, busy cleaning the few tables Ruby had jammed up against the walls—mostly, people held their drinks in their hands and scarfed down their meals standing around the rim of the dance floor so they didn't miss the action, so there wasn't much to clean up, really. The waiter waved back, and then Effie got down to the matter at hand.

"I'm just sayin', you might do better if you were a little more, y'know . . ." Deena stammered.

"Shy?" Effie teased. "Sugar-sweet like you?"

"Boys seem to like it," Deena said, shrinking back as if in defeat.

"Well, I'm not interested in boys, Deena," Effie said as she watched Curtis stroll from the bar and over to their table. Effie sat up in her seat and put her elbow on the table, leaning forward just a little to push her chest out. She flashed a wide-toothed grin when he handed her a highball, and slid a bottle of Coke over to Deena.

"What you two jawin' about?"

"Well, Curtis," Effie said, mockingly glancing down demurely. "Do you cheat on your wife like Mr. Jimmy Early?"

Deena gasped. "Effie!" She turned to Curtis. "I don't know her."

Effie dismissed Deena's shock with a wave of her hand. "Deena's right, it's really none of our business. We don't even know if you're married."

Curtis, his shoulders squared so that he looked miles tall standing over the girls, didn't move an inch. "I was married. It didn't work out."

Effie leaned into him. "Was she one of those teeny little tweety-birds like Deena here? Or do you prefer a real woman," she said, sitting up straight.

"Effie, now you stop it!" Deena demanded, turning red.

Curtis answered without hesitation, looking Effie straight in the eyes. "Actually, I was raised by two older sisters, and they're both just as real as you are."

Effie pulled out the seat next to her and patted it, beckoning Curtis to sit. "Well, why don't you tell me about them?"

Curtis cleared his throat and looked over his shoulder, then turned back to the women. "In a minute, ladies," he said, as he nodded to C.C., who'd walked up to the table and shook Curtis's hand.

"You ready?" Curtis asked.

"Do a bear pee in the woods?"

The two walked over to a nearby booth, where Marty was sitting with Jimmy, drinking whiskey.

"It ain't workin', Marty! Man, I remember when that faint, it used to kill 'em! Slay 'em in the aisles, man!" Jimmy said excitedly, clearly still reeling from the less-than-enthusiastic reception by the Detroit audience to his trademark fall out at the end of his hit, "Fake Your Way to the Top." There was a time when Jimmy would fall to the stage and women from two miles around would scream and cry as they tried to climb over "security," trying to touch his prone body—but not that night. "Too many other people doin' it now," he practically whined.

"Yeah, Jimmy," Marty said. "Everybody's doin' it now."

"But I was the first! You know that, don't you?"

"And you're still the first, Jimmy," Marty said, slapping his back. "You killed 'em tonight. It was beautiful. Beau-ti-ful!"

Jimmy sat back in his chair and sized Marty up. "You're full of shit, Marty," he said simply. "I need something, man. Something . . ." Just then, Lorrell switched by, grinning as she made her way over to the bar, where she promptly started flirting with one of the trumpet players. "Something like that," Jimmy said, pointing at Lorrell. "Lord have mercy! Mama!" he called out.

"What you need is a new sound," Curtis deadpanned. Jimmy had been staring at Lorrell so hard that he didn't notice Curtis and C.C. had walked up to the table.

Without missing a beat, Jimmy chimed in, a tinge of disgust in his voice: "No baby, I need a new Caddy. The one you sold me is leaking oil." Marty cackled; he and Jimmy dismissed Curtis and C.C. with a quickness, just turned back to their conversation like the men weren't even standing there.

C.C. shrunk a bit, but, resolute, Curtis continued. "Jimmy, you remember Effie's brother, C.C. He's a very talented young composer."

"Oh yeah," Jimmy said, looking up at C.C. and snapping his finger. "You wrote that song the girls do. How's it go? *'You betta move, move . . .'* You wrote that one, huh?"

C.C. squared his shoulders again. "With absolutely no help from anyone," he said proudly.

"What do you think of that song, Marty," Jimmy said, keeping his eyes on C.C.

"Well, I think it's kind of . . ."

"Boring?" Jimmy asked.

"Yeah. It's real boring, kid," Marty said, taking a sip of his whiskey.

C.C. narrowed his eyes like slits. "I'm no kid, mister," he said, slinking away.

"I'm sorry but that song just don't have enough soul in it, you know what I mean, baby? I'm Jimmy and I gotta have soul," he yelled out to no one in particular, just as the trumpet player up on the stage let a staccato riff soar. "Yeah," Jimmy yelled. "Gotta have soul, brothers!"

Curtis slid into the booth next to Jimmy. "Sure—soul and gospel, too. And R&B and jazz and blues and everything else the man has grabbed from us," Curtis said, borrowing from a lecture he'd given C.C. just a few days ago, after the two wrapped up an all-night songwriting session. The two had spent a lot of long nights together, writing songs on a used piano Curtis copped from a small local university that was looking to unload some old instruments. Curtis paid for it with his dealership cash, and promptly parked it in the cramped, dusty garage, with a promise from C.C., who for weeks had been trying to talk his sister's manager into signing him onto his roster as a songwriter, that he'd pay for the piano and then some by writing hits for the Dreamettes. Curtis liked two things about that boy—his energy, and his innocence, which meant he was hungry, just like Curtis. It didn't take Curtis but two sentences to convince C.C. to crank out more than a dozen original pop tunes during the three weeks the piano stood at attention in that garage, all while Curtis listened intently, changing chords here, stretching out notes there to come up with the hit that would put Jimmy, whom Curtis was desperate to add to his burgeoning new roster of talent, on the pop charts. C.C. drank in Curtis—respected him not only for his business acumen, but for his clear love of the music and for opening his mind to being more than just a second-rate R&B songwriter. And he wanted to be a part of Curtis's number—could see with crystal-clear clarity that what he and Curtis were doing would, someday, make history. Why, he didn't even get upset when Curtis changed his music—just listened and nodded and bent over the piano as Curtis strolled to and fro, firing ideas as C.C. played way into the night.

"There's got to be a way to bring our music to a broader audience," Curtis said, narrowing his eyes and leaning in toward Jimmy. "Only this time, with our artists. Our money."

Jimmy sized him up. "Marty, this man is handing me crap."

"Yeah, I know, baby," Marty said, laughing off Curtis. It was C.C.'s singing that wiped the smirk off his face.

"Got me a Cadillac, Cadillac, Cadillac/Got me a Cadillac car," he sang, plunking out a catchy tune on the house piano. The trumpet player put down his horn and leaned in a little closer, as Lorrell walked over and added a *"ooh ooh."*

"Got me a Cadillac, Cadillac, Cadillac/Look at me, mister, I'm a star!" he sang a little louder, as Deena and Effie joined in with Lorrell, as they'd done countless times before at Effie's house, when C.C. hammered out material for them to sing at local talent shows. It didn't take long for Jimmy to start tapping his foot to the infectious beat.

"Look, I know what you cats are trying to do and you can forget it," Marty said, pounding his fist on the table. He was all too clear that Curtis was out to stick him for his top—and only—artist. "Jimmy Early ain't some streetcorner punk looking for his first date. He's an established artist with a recording contract."

"On a weak local label that can't move his records to the pop charts," Curtis said smoothly.

"There's nothing we can do about that," Marty stammered, as Jimmy sat back, taking it all in.

Curtis shook his head and turned his attention to Jimmy. "One record, man. That's all I'm asking for. One song with a simple hook everyone can relate to. 'Look at my pretty car—it makes me feel like a movie star,' " he said in a singsongy voice.

Marty jumped up from the booth and reached for his coat and hat. Curtis smelled blood. "You know where all the hits happen these days? In cars, man! Songs that make you feel good while you're driving your automobile."

"Yeah, well, Jimmy's fans like to take the bus," Marty huffed. "Let's hit it, Jimmy," he said, holding up Jimmy's coat. Jimmy stood up and moved past Marty, toward the piano. Curtis smiled. Defeated, Marty took off his hat and dropped back down in his seat.

"Hey baby, you figure out the bridge yet?" Jimmy said to C.C., snapping his fingers as he sang the words, backed up by the girls' harmony.

"Okay, we'll go again." C.C. smiled, adjusting himself on the piano bench.

Not even twenty-four hours later, Jimmy and the girls were standing in the garage at Curtis's Cadillac dealership, crammed between a four-piece band and a wall full of homemade baffles. Curtis and Wayne, an older man whom Curtis called a salesman but worked like a personal assistant, sat at a metal tool desk, which they'd cleared to make room for a used two-track recorder and mixing board.

"It's soundin' a little tick-tock, boys," Curtis called out to the band. "Let's stay in the pocket. And Jimmy, easy on the church, brother. Nice and easy. We know you got soul, but for this song, I need you to sing nice and easy."

Curtis nodded to Wayne. "Hold the work!" Wayne called out to the repairman at the other end of the garage, who was in the middle of spray-painting a fender on a freshly painted black Cadillac; Curtis had hired him special to jazz it up. "Record 'Cadillac Car.' Take nine," Wayne said.

C.C. shook tire chains to accentuate the backbeat, and then Jimmy burst into song, the Dreamettes swaying behind him, punctuating his notes with sweet *"oohs,"* and pearly *"Cadillacs."* At the mixing board, Curtis smoothed out the sound, dialing down the trumpets and boosting the vocal. He flicked a switch, which crunched the mix through two small speakers, making the song sound as if it was flowing through a tinny car radio. Jimmy nodded his head and threw himself into the song.

Two nights later, C.C. and Wayne were in the parking lot of A&B Distributors, loading up Curtis's gold Cadillac with the first boxes of "Cadillac Car." C.C. was practically bubbling in the backseat as the trio rode over to WAMK, where Curtis was set to do some fast talking to convince Elvis

Kelly, a popular local deejay, to drop the needle on the newly pressed 45, stamped "Property of Rainbow Records." He suspected, though, that once Elvis heard the hit, it wouldn't be too hard to get the deejay to yield.

"Curtis, why are we riding around in this car like we ain't got nowhere to go? All this snow coming down?" Effie demanded from the backseat of his Cadillac, where she was sitting squished between Deena and Lorrell. C.C. was riding shotgun. Curtis didn't answer, just turned up the radio and kept driving. Effie had been fussing so that they didn't hear Elvis's introduction: "Let me get a hold of your ear," he shouted into his mic. "This is a different sound for the Thunder Man, and I think you're gonna enjoy it." But she didn't have any words when she heard Jimmy's voice ring out above hers and the girls. They erupted.

"Curtis, we're on the radio!" Effie screamed, throwing her arms around him. Just then, the sound broke up.

"What's happening," Lorrell said, her eyes going wide as saucers.

"Black station . . . the signal's too weak," C.C. said. He fiddled with the dial, but the song was gone.

"Curtis, turn this boat around. Hurry up!"

Effie demanded, smacking him on the arm. The car swerved as he negotiated an exaggerated U-turn on a patch of ice. As soon as the car was pointed toward the city, the song came back. The girls started singing along, giggling and yelling between notes.

And that was the beginning of their climb up the charts. But a lot of sweat went into the success of that song; Curtis, Lorrell, Effie, Deena, C.C., and Wayne became the marketers, distributors, and chief cheerleaders of "Cadillac Car," which hit number eight on the R&B charts and ninty-eight on the pop charts within the first week—the latter unheard of for a soulful black artist who usually gyrated and screamed his way through his numbers. With their dedication to Rainbow Records and its first and only hit, "Cadillac Car" peaked at number thirty-eight on *Billboard*'s pop charts.

They were bona fide stars—couldn't nobody tell them nothin'.

THREE

Fire was in C.C.'s eyes—his legs trembled but he couldn't bring himself to sit down, even as Effie gently rubbed his back and swore to him over and over and over yet again that somebody was "gonna pay." But C.C. knew better than that. White boys never paid when they took from Negroes, because in 1963, nobody considered that stealing. And so C.C. got his recourse the only way he possibly could at that moment in time—by picking up the first thing his hands could grab and throwing it with all his might at the TV set, which was tuned into young America's favorite television show, *American Bandstand.* C.C.'s ire was directed at the show's featured guest, Dave and the Sweethearts, the very blond, very thin, very white group that enjoyed frequent write-ups in *Billboard* and plenty more airtime on white pop radio stations; Dave and the girls were performing what Dick Clark described as "their marvelous new recording, 'Cadillac Car.' " The glass full of pop shattered against Dave's stiff-moving body; the liquid dripped all across the Sweethearts' faces and down their tight dresses. Palm trees swayed against the glorious sky that enveloped the group's stage set, unaffected by the sudden shower of cola.

"C.C.!" Effie yelled as Lorrell rushed over to the TV and shut it off. "You gonna electrocute all our asses in here, tossing soda on that electric set!"

"Damn the TV, Effie—that white boy was singing my song. *My* song!" C.C. said, swinging his fists at the air for emphasis. "Can't believe this!" He rushed for the front door and snatched it open. All three girls jumped when he slammed it behind him. They could hear his car engine roar and his tires screeching across the parking lot as he sped off into the night.

Curtis heard C.C.'s brakes squealing to a stop in the lot, but he kept staring ahead, taking long drags on his cigarette. Wayne, who watched the lanky 17-year-old slam his car door and stomp across the pavement to the front office, got up from his chair and moved closer to Curtis, a look of concern emphasizing the creases around his eyes.

"How can they do that? It's my song, Curtis. Our song," C.C. demanded as he burst through the door and stood over Curtis. Unmoved, Curtis continued to stare past C.C., blowing smoke into the stale air.

"Marty says it happens all the time," Wayne said, shaking his head. "Once something is out there . . ."

"That's bull," C.C. said, cutting off Wayne's shucking. "He should have protected us. They stole our hit. I never thought . . ."

Curtis looked away, the mention of Marty's name searing him to the core. "Forget Marty. You got me to think for you now," Curtis said, slowly standing up, his body within inches of C.C.'s, a move that made C.C. shrink back. Then, lowering his voice, Curtis added: "Everything is under control."

Just then, the phone rang. Curtis snatched the handset off the receiver, and said, "Yeah," then listened without saying another word for a good minute. Finally, he said, "Right," and gently hung up the phone. Picking up his suit jacket off the back of his chair, Curtis headed for the door and held it open. "Go home. Be here first thing in the morning—and wear a suit. We got work to do."

Confused, but too apprehensive to ask any questions, C.C. slowly walked toward the door, looking first at Wayne, then at Curtis, then at the floor. He might have been young, but C.C. was smart enough to know when to shut the hell up and do as told. He considered Curtis a mentor, and even though the car dealer's experience in the music industry was about as limited as his, C.C. had a feeling that if he just hung in there, Curtis would figure out a way to get the young songwriter his just due, and then some.

C.C. noticed the banner first—couldn't help but see it, considering how it filled the dealership's entire glass front window. It read, "Close-Out Sale—Everything Must Go." He parked his car on the street, hopped out, and stood by, watching with a look of confusion on his face as Curtis shook hands with a young black couple and handed them the keys to a new cream-colored Caddy, which Wayne was pulling out for them. The couple practically skipped over to their vehicle. C.C. caught Wayne's attention and gestured a what's-going-on? shrug. Wayne just tossed his chin in Curtis's direction and moved on to another customer, this one an older man in a dapper suit who'd been eyeing a used red car C.C.'d seen being fixed up just a few days before.

Curtis waved C.C. into the office and told him to take a seat. "Here's what you're going to do:

Anybody who comes in here looking to buy a car will not leave here without a set of keys in his hand—understand me?" Curtis said. "I want every one of these cars off this lot in the next ten days."

"But what about your business—" C.C. started.

"Music is my business now," Curtis cut him off. "And I—we—can't make music here at the headquarters of Rainbow Records if we got to stand around trying to convince people to buy up these cars. My lead songwriter and musical director can't do his job in the middle of that," he said, slapping C.C.'s back. "Now what I need you to do is go out there and clear off that lot. Get to it, now."

A grin slowly spread across C.C.'s face. Hot damn, he thought. In all the years he'd been writing his songs, with all the prayers he'd sent up asking God to help him get his music out, C.C. never really thought he'd have a bona fide shot at hearing one of his pieces anywhere but at the Motor City Revue and the occasional wedding or graduation party the Dreamettes sang at. But in just over three months, Curtis had changed his life by getting his hit record onto the radio—not only because he liked C.C.'s work, but because he, too, was passionate about music and how it inspired. They'd sit for hours over the piano, tinkering with notes and deliberating over words—arguing about who was better, Billie Holiday (Curtis's favorite) or Sarah Vaughn (C.C.'s idol). No one had ever come close to being as fanatical about music, or recognizing that C.C. had what it took to get his music heard on a national level. No one. And he could feel it in his gut that Curtis had some bigger plans to come.

C.C. nodded at his new boss, clapped his hands together, and walked out onto the lot. He eyed a couple checking out the green beauty Effie had admired whenever she came by Curtis's dealership. "Ain't she a beauty?" C.C. asked, walking up to the couple. "I can get you a real nice price on it."

It took them only seven days to clear out that lot; as the last car drove off, Curtis flipped the switch on a new sign, which lit up to read, "Rainbow Records—The Sound of Tomorrow." He stood in the door with a cigarette dangling in his mouth. "C.C., go on over to the piano and play that song you was working on—that one, how it go? *Steppin', steppin', steppin' to the bad side,*" he said. "I got some business we need to take care of tonight, but I want Jimmy and the girls over here first thing in the morning so we can record that. Whatever changes we need to make to it, we need to do it now," he said, picking up a briefcase and walking over to the desk at which Wayne was sitting. "Wayne, help me count this out," he said, plopping the briefcase on the metal workspace. He popped open the top to reveal stacks and stacks of cash. C.C. had to hold his breath so as not to gasp out loud—it looked like play money to him, there was so much there. He tried to avert his stare, but it was useless. Curtis smirked. "Go on, git over there and bang me out a hit, boy."

More than two hours had passed by the time Curtis and Wayne counted their way through all that money, sorted it out in piles, and wrapped rubber bands around them. Curtis made a few trips over to the piano to fiddle with some of the lyrics and chord changes for "Steppin' to the Bad Side," but seemed to be quite pleased with the final product by the time he finished neatly stacking the money back into the briefcase.

"Come on, let's take a ride," Curtis said to C.C. as he headed for the door. "Wayne, close up for me, will you?"

"Sure thing, boss," Wayne and C.C. said in unison.

C.C. didn't have a bank account so he wasn't one hundred percent sure, but he'd always thought banks closed in the late afternoon, so he didn't quite understand where they were headed with all that money in the trunk of the car. Curtis wasn't offering up any information—just drove in silence past countless financial institutions and through backstreets full of abandoned, boarded-up buildings, the sight of which made C.C. quite uneasy. Something wasn't right. And though the dull ache in the pit of his stomach beckoned him to keep his mouth shut, C.C. couldn't help but ask, "So, where we going, boss?"

"Going to take care of some business," Curtis said simply.

"I know, boss, but we got a suitcase full of money back there, and we been driving around this shady neighborhood for longer than a minute now, and—"

"Look, youngblood, there's some things you're going to have to learn to get ahead in this business, and I'm willing to teach you, but you gonna have to watch and learn instead of talking, right?"

"Yeah, I understand boss, but—"

"But you want a game plan, huh?" Curtis asked, turning to look at C.C.

"I mean, I feel like I'm about to be a part of something big here, Curtis, and I want to learn from you. You a successful businessman and all that and I'm just saying I want to learn."

"Wanna learn, huh?" Curtis said, smirking.

"Yes, sir," C.C. said, a little bit more strongly.

Curtis was silent for a moment. "Well learn this:

We're taking a ride over to some friends of mine who are gonna help us get your new single onto the radio—but not just any radio station, youngblood. I'm talking them white stations. All across the country," Curtis said finally. "They got connections in cities we ain't never seen before—the important places, Atlanta, New York, L.A., Dallas, Miami. And I don't mean connections with the black deejays. I mean connections with the people who put people on the map—the *American Bandstand* map," he said as he pulled into a parking lot in the back of an industrial warehouse. The lights were dim, the area desolate; C.C. didn't know where the hell he was. Curtis shut off the motor, reached into his jacket pocket, pulled out his wallet, and took out a crisp one-hundred-dollar bill. "Let's go," he said, as he got out of the car and headed for the trunk.

That C-note came in real handy at the back door of that warehouse, where a burly bouncer in a fantastically well-tailored suit stood sentry. C.C. didn't like the looks of him; the man made him nervous—not just because he looked like he was probably up to no good, but because he was a white man who looked like he was up to no good, the worst kinda white boy to find yourself around in the dark back alleys of racially intolerant Detroit. C.C. wanted to stand tall to send the message he wasn't scared, but he couldn't help but inch a little closer to Curtis. The bouncer snapped the bill, folded it in half, and tucked it into his pocket, then opened the doors to the freight elevator, inviting Curtis and C.C. to step on. They descended to a leaky, dark warehouse floor that was empty save for a couple of desks, a long table, and a shady-looking white man with silvering hair and gut damn near bursting his shirt buttons. Curtis slid the briefcase across the man's desk.

"Who the hell is this?" the man said, pointing to C.C.

"Who this?" Curtis asked. "That's C.C., the hitmaker."

"Uh, nice . . . nice to meet you," C.C. stammered, extending his hand.

The man ignored him, and instead opened the suitcase, looked in, and nodded. "I leave in three days," he said. "You'll have what I need by then?"

"Not a problem," Curtis said.

"See you then," the man said.

It was C.C. who carried the boxes of 45s to Nicky Cassaro, who, C.C. later learned, delivered "Steppin' to the Bad Side," to each of his "friends" in cities throughout the country, with a "thank-you note" or two from Curtis's briefcase—a small token of appreciation, Cassaro told C.C., for spinning Jimmy's hit on their radio shows. C.C. didn't think much of it; sure, Nicky and his henchmen made him nervous, but he figured this was standard procedure if you wanted your music to get into the right hands. At least that's what Curtis told him, and C.C. believed it.

Needless to say, the deejays expressed their gratitude in ways that, a mere month later, made even the seemingly unaffected Curtis get worked up. "Number fifteen. On the pop chart!" he yelled, rushing into Rainbow Records, waving *Billboard* over his head. "With a bullet!"

C.C., who'd been rehearsing a group of fourteen dancers for Jimmy's new stage show, stopped mid-hip swivel when he realized what Curtis had just said.

"Number fifteen?" he said, rushing over to Curtis and snatching the *Billboard* from his hands. "Where is it—what page?"

"Eleven," Curtis said, turning off the record player, which had been cranking "Steppin' to the Bad Side" from the set of used speakers C.C. had borrowed from the recording studio to rehearse.

C.C. hurriedly flipped through the pages, barely able to contain his excitement. There it was, "Steppin' to the Bad Side," sandwiched in on the Hot 100 list by Bobby Rydell's "Wildwood Days," and the Surfaris' "Wipe Out." His song's title was followed by Jimmy's name, and then, in parentheses, his name and Curtis's. The sight of it made C.C.'s knees buckle. Curtis interrupted his elation.

"Now look, C.C., we got to strike with this thing while it's smokin'," he said, pacing in front of the record player. "I've already been in touch with a few people and I scored Jimmy a gig at the Apollo. June 23. We'll leave here next Friday—that'll give us a week to get there, rehearse the numbers on the stage, and get ready."

"June 23?" C.C. asked, his face falling. "Damn."

"What, man?" Curtis said, annoyed that C.C. wasn't showing the proper excitement for his big news. The Apollo, after all, was the crown jewel of chitlin' circuit theatres—the Big Apple the place where all their song heroes had found their voices and gone on to stardom. Billie, Sarah, Ella, Little Anthony, Chuck Berry, Ray Charles—they'd all danced across that stage, used their voices to chew up the tough crowd that filled those seats. And now Curtis had scored a spot for Jimmy, who would be singing C.C.'s song. And this Negro was asking questions?

"Nothing," C.C. said, recognizing his blunder. "It's nothing, really," he said. "It's just that me and a couple of guys in the band were planning on going to the march over to Cobo Hall on June 23."

"March?" Curtis asked, genuinely perplexed. "Is walking up and down the street going to put money in your pocket?"

"Well, naw, man," C.C. stammered. "But seems to me like we all should have some kind of interest in keeping The Man off our asses while we trying to make it. I mean, Martin Luther King, Jr.'s going to be marching right past this storefront—it's going to be part of history."

"Listen, The Man's going to be too busy using his feet to dance to your music to care about putting it in your ass," Curtis said. "If you want to go down in history, keep writing those hit records. People don't forget a good song. Just get back to rehearsing and put together the show this hit—your hit—deserves." And with that, he switched on the record player and put the needle on the round, black disc.

C.C. slowly turned back to the dancers, who'd already gotten into formation behind him, their bodies reflecting in the mirrors propped up against the wall. He couldn't agree with Curtis's notion that the fight could be fought with a few hit records—someone had to be down with the struggle, and plenty more had to be willing to hit the frontlines if true change was going to come. But this much C.C.

knew: He also had a job, and that job was to prepare for their big break, and if that meant missing Dr. King this time around, then it was the sacrifice he had to make. So C.C. tossed the *Billboard* onto the metal table and gazed at it one more time. Had he taken a few minutes to read through it, he would have seen the story on page 3, about a rash of violent assaults on radio station managers in Atlanta, Dallas, and Miami—beatings, the police and the reporter speculated, that may have been tied to an illegal payola scheme to get radio airplay for some of the country's hottest records. The police didn't have any leads on who was responsible for the violence. But Curtis did, and it would have been crystal clear to C.C. "Five, six, seven, eight," C.C. yelled, before hopping to the left, spinning, then thrusting his hips forward—the dancers mimicking his steps. C.C. watched them move in synch with the rhythm.

Needless to say, C.C. wasn't thinking about no Martin Luther King, Jr., and his historic Detroit Freedom Rally when he was standing backstage at the Apollo, where a rumbling crowd of jaded New Yorkers were treating Jimmy, the Dreamettes, and their entourage like they were a bunch of no-count, 'Bama ass country folk who didn't deserve to grace the legendary stage. Even the man at the stage door, who presumably had been told to expect the performer who had the number one song in the country, greeted them with a "Who you and what y'all want?" when Curtis offered his hand and started to introduce Jimmy. Their tepid reception, and the reputation of the Apollo audience as one that would not hesitate to boo even their own mamas off the stage if the women who birthed them didn't come with it, had everyone, even Jimmy, on edge.

"You sure them dancers got the steps?" Jimmy asked Marty as he paced his dressing room floor. " 'Cause they got to be all the way right, jack. That's a fact."

Marty, anxious to hold on to his small-and-ever-dwindling control over Jimmy by appealing to his ego, made yet another futile attempt to dress down the changes Curtis and C.C. made to his client's show. "I'm just saying, brother, make sure your moves are on point, because I wouldn't have just left your show to no bunch of amateurs," Marty said. "One screwup from them and that's your ass out there." Marty didn't realize Curtis was standing behind him.

"Don't you worry about the dancers," Curtis said, pulling on his cigarette and tossing his fedora on the vanity. "C.C., the dancers, the girls, they're all ready to get out there and show the Apollo Jimmy 'Thunder' Early means business, baby."

Effie, Lorrell, and Deena rushed into the dressing room, a gaggle of hairdressers and makeup artists with combs and blush brushes and powder in their wake. "Have mercy, you see that crowd out there?" Effie asked excitedly. "I ain't seen folks dressed like that since Easter Sunday."

"Yeah, well, they ain't actin' like church folks out there," Lorrell said. "Did you see how they booed that last group off the stage?"

"That's what they're supposed to do," Curtis interjected. "It's a talent show. But y'all are part of the headliner. You backing up a star. Don't forget that."

"Y'all come on now, we ain't got all night," the announcer yelled through the door, rapping his knuckles on the wood like he was going to put his fist through it.

Jimmy looked at the girls and over at the musicians, then C.C., Curtis, and finally, Marty. "Y'all know Jimmy don't pray, but I'm half tempted to send up some timber over this one," he said. And then he walked out the door.

"Ladies and gentlemen! Please welcome to the Apollo Theatre's legendary stage—Jimmy Early and the Dreamettes, singing their number one hit, 'Steppin' to the Bad Side,' " the announcer yelled into the microphone. The heavy purple curtains swooshed open to reveal the dancers; the Dreamettes exploded onto the stage behind them, working their bodies in a dancing fury to ratchet up the crowd's reaction. The audience erupted into applause and cheers, and then practically detonated when Jimmy skipped onto the stage. *"I had to step into the bad side!"* he wailed.

Curtis watched from the wings, pounding the floor to the driving music. *I did it,* he thought, his heart filled with pride. It was clear that he'd hit upon something, that everything was about to change for him, for Jimmy and the girls, for C.C., for the music industry. He was about to go down in history as the architect of a new era for black music artists. *I made this happen.*

Marty watched impassively. He knew what was up. This show was the beginning of his end with Jimmy.

The master tape snaked its way through the open reel deck as the audio signal fed into the record cutter. Like a knife to soft butter, it cut grooves into the rotating disc of acetate lacquer as Martin Luther King, Jr.'s voice filled the room.

"The motor's now cranked up and we're moving up the highway of freedom toward the city of equality . . ." King said, as yet another soft lump of hot vinyl dropped onto the stamper, which shaped the record and pressed on the center label:

"Dr. Martin Luther King, Jr., 1963 Detroit Freedom Rally, Cobo Hall." "And we can't afford to stop now because our nation has a date with destiny! We must keep moving!" King's voice rang out.

The King album in hand, Effie headed through the Rainbow Records garage, which by now was a beehive of activity. "I made my peach cobbler, Effie!" Aunt Ethel called out from the kitchen, but Effie, already on a mission and the move, marched right past, and stormed into Curtis's office, where Curtis was playing the King album for his sisters, Rhonda and Janice.

"Curtis!" she said.

He looked up and cocked an eyebrow. "Effie, you know my sis—" he started.

Effie cut him off. "Tell me something. Do you think it's right to promote an amateur performer over a professional?"

Curtis lifted the needle from the record; Rhonda and Janice looked at each other as Effie continued to light into their brother.

"I'm not sure what this is about," he said.

"It's about fairness, Curtis. It's about people paying their dues. Isn't that what you keep telling me? 'Get in line, Effie. Wait your turn,' " she said mockingly.

"Yeah, well I guess . . ." Curtis started again, finally realizing where this was heading. Effie had started hammering away at him, of late, demanding every chance she could that her manager/kinda-sorta boyfriend—yes, Curtis and Effie, still high from their triumphant Harlem reception, had taken it there while heading back to Detroit from the Apollo—give her a shot at a solo. "Just one song," she'd say every chance she'd get him hemmed up in somebody's corner, and, of late, even in front of the other girls. Curtis was in no mood for that discussion again.

"So why am I sitting here without so much as a B side on a 45 when an amateur like Martin Luther King, Jr., gets his own friggin' album?" Effie demanded.

Curtis, trying to figure out a way to respond to the outrageousness of Effie's argument without setting her off, turned to his sisters, his eyes begging for help.

"I mean, can he even sing?" Effie said, her hands on her hips. Not even a moment later, Effie, Rhonda, and Janice burst into laughter, their way of letting Curtis know that he'd been had. Effie leaned down and put her arms around Curtis. "You're a great man, Curtis," she said sweetly. "Isn't your brother a great man?"

Curtis leaned in and kissed Effie, a soft, passionate peck that made clear to their public that their relationship had, indeed, developed into something much more. What, exactly, the "more" was, was still up for debate. Effie thought they were headed toward an official relationship. Curtis, never one to turn away some tail—thought it made it easier for him to keep Effie busy while he worked on building up the label. His next act, after all, had to stand up to Jimmy's showmanship and sex appeal, and though Effie hadn't a problem showing her ass, Curtis just didn't think she had what it took to become a crossover sensation. Too much church in her voice—and much too much meat on her bones, he decided. He also understood pretty quickly that it would be easier to make Effie think he was her man than it would be to tell her she didn't look the part of Rainbow Records' next big talent.

"Hey baby, why don't you go and find C.C. and work on that song y'all been writing," he said. "I need to get out here and see how Wayne's doing with finding me a secretary."

"Don't look too hard," Effie said, leaning in for another smooch before she headed off toward the recording studio.

Curtis pushed himself up from his chair and headed to the office, which was, by now, mobbed with various musical acts—so many that they were spilling out into the parking lot. They swarmed around him when they realized who Curtis was.

"Whoa," Curtis said, moving back, his eyes searching for Wayne, who was being feted with hard-luck stories and pleas from the multitudes of artists trying to convince him they deserved a deal with Rainbow Records. Curtis raised his hands, beckoning the crowd to calm itself. "I promise we'll get to all of you, but right now I need someone who can answer the phone," Curtis said. "Anyone here have any secretarial experience?"

A young woman, with almond-shaped eyes the same color as her light brown skin, pushed her way through the crowd. "I can do it," she said confidently.

Curtis glanced at her fingers, which sported inch-long synthetic nails. How was she going to take dictation, file, and type up contracts with those? Curtis raised an eyebrow; she started ripping her nails off, one by one.

"Okay, okay, you got the job," Curtis said. "Wayne? Show Miss . . . um, what's your name?"

"Michelle Morris," she squealed.

Curtis laughed. "Okay, Miss Morris. You come with me," he said, then turned to the crowd. "Everybody, thanks for stopping in. Wayne will be right with you—he'll get to each and every one of you. Rainbow Records welcomes you to the sound of tomorrow!"

Curtis popped his head into the recording studio to grab C.C., who was playing the piano while his sister slinked her way through a song her brother had written for her. When she saw Curtis, she put a little extra into the words—*"You're strong and you're smart/You've taken my heart/And I'll give you the rest of me, too,"* she sang, looking Curtis in his eyes. A smile slowly spread across his face as she kept singing. He let out a little laugh. "Hey um, hate to interrupt, especially that one," he said, "but, C.C., I need you in the showroom, baby." And then to Effie: "I'll bring him right back," he said.

C.C. and Michelle followed him into the showroom, where Rhonda and Janice sat, sewing and stitching gowns just beyond a sheet they'd hung to separate the conference area from the changing station, where Deena was busy squeezing into a slinky silver number. "All right," Curtis said. "I need your opinion on this. I'm picking the cover art for the new album, and I want y'all to tell me which one of these albums you'd pick up in a record store."

C.C. and Michelle leaned in, but Curtis snatched back the mock-ups. "But," he said, "not the record store in the 'hood. I'm talking about the one over there in one of them white neighborhoods." Then he held up the covers. One was of Jimmy leaning into a microphone with the girls standing behind him, admiring the singer. The next was a picture of a man and three women in silhouette, their faces and clothes so dark, they looked almost like shadows. The third, a line drawing of a fun guy and three sexy chicks—all of indeterminate race, was Curtis's final sample. Michelle nodded at it approvingly; Curtis was about to ask C.C. his thoughts when Deena stepped from behind the sheet wearing a long, tight gown that flared at the knees—her beanpole figure filled out with hip pads and a padded bra Rhonda had sewn in it at Curtis's request. Curtis stared, surprised at how beautiful Deena had become. Even as she twirled in the mirror, Curtis kept staring, and soon Deena caught hold of his gaze. She turned so he could see more.

C.C., still looking over the mock covers, was oblivious to the mini fashion show, but Rhonda and Janice saw it all, and exchanged looks. Down the hallway, they could hear Effie singing C.C.'s song; by the time she made it into the showroom, she was belting the words, singing them directly to Curtis: *"I'm here when you call/You've got it all/And confidence like I never knew./You're the perfect man for me/And love you, I do."*

"All right now," Janice said. "You betta sing that song."

"C.C. wrote it for me," Effie said as she took Curtis's hand.

"What do you think, Curtis," C.C. said, finally looking up from the covers.

"It's got a good hook, but it's still too light," Curtis said. "We want it light, but not that light."

C.C., taken aback by Curtis's quick and curt dismissal of a piece he'd worked so hard on, slunk down in his chair, defeated. Still, he wasn't up for arguing with Curtis about it—not with such a huge audience. Maybe, he thought, he'd bring it up another time, when just the two of them were in the studio. Maybe.

"Okay . . ." Effie said. "But if we fix it, it's going in the show, right?"

"First things first. I gotta get Jimmy booked into Miami, even if it means buying our own hotel," Curtis said, trying to change the subject.

"But you promised I wouldn't spend my life singing backup, Curtis."

"And you won't, baby. You think I'm going to let a voice like yours go to waste?" he said. Looking to avoid eye contact with Effie, Curtis's eyes landed on Deena's. She smiled, and went back behind the sheet.

Seeing movement out the corner of his eye, Curtis glanced out the window to see Marty jumping out of his car in the parking lot and slamming the door.

"Effie, you're just going to have to trust me," he said to her, though his attention was on Marty.

"Can we talk about it more tonight?" Effie asked.

"Sure. Tonight," Curtis said, as he headed out the door.

Marty moved toward Curtis. "Boy, you a real snake! A cheap, second-rate hustler, nothing but a streetcorner con artist!" Marty yelled.

"Marty, whatever this is about, let's take it into my office . . ."

"I'm away a week and you're canceling dates behind my back?" he said, cutting Curtis off. "I spent six months setting up that tour for Jimmy!"

"Jimmy's too big for that chitlin' circuit mess. I think I can get him booked into the Paradise in Miami Beach," Curtis said, maintaining his composure.

"Miami?" Marty said, incredulous. "You really are drifting out there, chump! You couldn't even get Sammy Davis, Jr. in there. That place is so white, they don't even let our boys park the cars."

"I just got him an audition," Curtis said simply.

Marty was taken aback by the news. "Luck, man. Hustler's luck," he said dismissively.

"And Miami's just the beginning," Curtis said, ignoring the insult. "There's no reason Jimmy can't be playing the Copa, the Americana, even *American Bandstand.*"

"I been in this business too many years to listen to some hotshot talking bull," Marty said, snatching off his hat.

"Not bull—change," Curtis said. "I'm talking change. Look around you, man. The time is now! But Jimmy needs a new act. Something classier, with a catchier sound."

"That'll go down better with a white audience?" Marty asked, smirking.

"That will put him where he should be, making the kind of money he should be making," Curtis said, raising his voice just a bit. "Jimmy's on the pop charts now. He's hot. We can do this for him."

"We? We ain't got to do nothing," Marty yelled. "Jimmy's mine. So back off, Curtis. Jimmy's mine."

Neither of them had seen Jimmy walk up behind Marty. "Jimmy," he said, "don't belong to no one."

Marty spun around. "Are you defending this car salesman, Jimmy?" he seethed. "Can't you see he's using you?"

"Ain't nobody usin' Jimmy! Nobody," Jimmy insisted.

"Who you think you're talking to, baby?" Marty said, almost whispering. "This is Marty. The man who found you singing for pennies when you were ten years old."

"Yeah, well, Marty," Jimmy opined, "it's a different time now. And a different Jimmy."

Marty shook his head and then spun around on his heels to face Curtis. "You want him, brother? You got him. I'm through," he said, before pushing past Jimmy and out to his car.

"Now look—" Jimmy started.

"You can't have it all, baby," Marty called over his shoulder.

"Please, Marty. I don't want you to go," Jimmy said.

"I love you, Jimmy, but you can't have it all," Marty called over his shoulder.

"Let's get back to work," Curtis said. But both he and Jimmy watched as Marty put on his hat and climbed into his old Plymouth. Jimmy, who'd been the best of friends with Marty for years, was devastated.

FOUR

"Happeee biiirth-daaay toooo you," Jimmy, Effie, and Deena harmonized as Lorrell stood over a cake with her name and a huge "18" written in pink across the icing. Grinning like a four-year-old about to plunge her finger into the thick confection, Lorrell clapped and squeaked and blew out the candles, to the applause of her friends.

"Did you make a wish, baby?" Jimmy said slyly.

"I sure did," Lorrell said, her smile betraying the naughty thoughts that had, the moment they left for Miami Beach, pervaded her mind. She couldn't get Jimmy out of her head. Specifically, she couldn't stop thinking about what Jimmy whispered into her ear the night they pulled out from Detroit: "You young now, baby, but when you turn eighteen, you all Jimmy's," he'd said as she snuggled into his chest. "You gonna be full grown and ready for Jimmy, ain't you? I'ma wait real patient. Jimmy can wait."

"What, all of three days, huh?" She'd laughed.

"Shoot, that's too long for me, but lucky for you I'm a patient man. But don't keep me waiting too long, hear?"

Now, there they were, standing in the living area of Miss Barbara's three-story tenement, which she'd smartly turned into a luxurious hotel where Negro acts, barred from the whites-only hotel strip by the beach, kicked up their heels while they waited for their chance to perform. Jimmy had been whispering and humming "Happy Birthday" to Lorrell all day, and making a big deal out of her being "a woman now." She knew full well what that meant to Jimmy, but now, she wasn't sure she was ready to hand over her virginity to the married singer, who struggled so with being away from his wife and refused by his teenage girlfriend, that he openly flaunted the fact that he was regularly getting sex from groupies. Lorrell threatened to confront him about it once, but an unlikely advocate—Effie—took Jimmy's defense. "Girl, Jimmy's a grown man and grown men have needs. And when men like Jimmy need it, they get it. It ain't got nothing to do with you. Now when you stop holding out on him, then you can make some demands on where he puts his pecker.

But until then, just turn your head and remember that until you ready to give it up, the only woman got claims on Jimmy Early is Mrs. Early."

Well, by the time she blew out the candles on her cake, Lorrell knew she was ready to be more than just Jimmy's girl. And, as if a sign from the Creator himself, when she opened her eyes, Jimmy was kneeling in front of her, with a small box resting in his palm. Lorrell eagerly took the box and unwrapped it, then squealed with delight. There was a collective gasp in the room when she held up the emerald ring, the rock as big as her knuckle. Lorrell jumped up and down as she helped Jimmy up; before he could get on his feet, Lorrell fell onto his lips, giving him a deep kiss that made his spine tingle.

Their embrace was interrupted by Deena, who quietly tipped down the stairs but cleared her throat as she made her grand entrance. "I'm so sorry I'm late," she said, walking over to Lorrell and giving her air kisses on each cheek.

"Well, that's what happens when you change four times," Effie shot back, looking at her fingernails.

Deena shot her a look, but shook off Effie's comment. As she hugged Lorrell, Effie walked over to Curtis, blocking his view of the whole affair. "Curtis, is it true you cried the first time you heard Billie Holiday sing?" she said, pushing her chest out and grinning up into his face.

"Now I wonder who told you that," he said, tossing a glance over in the direction of his sisters, Rhonda and Janice, who were sharing a laugh.

"Well, maybe you can tell me for yourself upstairs," she said, taking his hand. Curtis didn't hesitate—just let Effie lead him toward the staircase without another word.

Jimmy, watching them retire, turned back to Lorrell. "Hey baby, what do you say you get me and you a piece of that cake and some champagne to go," he whispered in her ear.

"Well, where we going?" she asked.

Jimmy simply motioned with his chin toward the staircase. Lorrell was growing ever more nervous. "Okay—why don't you meet me up there? I'll be along directly," she said, trying to avert her eyes from his.

"Don't keep me waiting too long, hear? I want me a piece of that cake," Jimmy whispered as he walked away.

It took Lorrell a good fifteen minutes to make it up those stairs, what with her stalling to show off her ring to Deena and offering to help Miss Barbara wash up the dishes and clean up the mess from the birthday party and pretending to thumb through a newspaper story announcing a speech

Martin Luther King, Jr., made during what the paper called the "March on Washington." When Deena finally retired to her room, and Miss Barbara was satisfied that no one else needed anything, and C.C. left to sit in with the house band at a colored club near their hotel, Lorrell finally worked up enough strength to carry her trembling legs up to the third floor. She hesitated before lightly tapping on Jimmy's door. It opened almost instantaneously, as if he were already standing there, just waiting. He pulled her into the room and quietly shut the door. "Where you been, sweet pea? I thought you wasn't never gonna come up here with my cake."

"Oh gosh, Jimmy, I forgot the cake downstairs. Let me go get you a slice," Lorrell said, starting for the door.

Jimmy took her hand off the knob and pulled her close to him. "Naw baby, that's okay. I'd rather taste you," he said, leaning in for a kiss.

Lorrell bobbed and ducked away from Jimmy, moving closer to his desk. He had sheet music spread out across it, as well as his toiletry bag, which was open just wide enough for Lorrell to see his stash of cocaine zipped into a little plastic baggie. Just beyond the wall, she could hear Effie moaning—and something tapping gently against the wall. Embarrassed by the noise of her best friend's lovemaking, Lorrell moved away from the wall like it was on fire, only to run smack into Jimmy, who she didn't realize was standing just behind her.

"Come on baby, you not scared of a little lovin', are you?" he said, running the back of his hand down her cheek. He cupped her chin into his hand and sweetly kissed her lips, then lunged into her mouth in earnest. Lorrell pushed him away.

"I ain't scared," she stammered. "This is all just happening a little fast."

"Don't worry, baby, I'll take my time . . ."

"I'm not a baby," Lorrell said, cutting him off. "I'm a woman now."

"I know you are," Jimmy said, his words almost punctuated with Effie's squeals. "And I'm a man. And all I want is to love you the way a man loves a woman," he said, leading her over to the bed. Lorrell looked at it nervously, and then back at Jimmy.

"I . . . I never done this before," she stammered.

"Shh . . . I know," he said, kissing her lips as he reached behind her and slowly unzipped her dress. Lorrell looked down and away, but Jimmy pulled her face back toward his. "Unbutton my shirt, while I help you out of your dress—nice and easy."

After they finished making love, Lorrell burst into tears. He planted gentle kisses all over her face, and shushed her as she held her hand over her mouth, her weak attempt to stave off her hysteria. "Shh, baby, come on, it's gonna be okay," Jimmy said, still kissing her. She turned her back to him, but he moved in closer to her body, spooning and comforting her as she sobbed into her pillow.

"You mine, baby—it's official. And I'm all yours, you hear? It's me and you now."

Lorrell, comforted by the idea of being Jimmy Early's girl, swiped at the tears rolling down her cheeks and smiled. "Oh Jimmy," she said as she leaned in to kiss her man.

By then, Effie had settled into Curtis's bed, too. But he had something other than love on his mind.

The manager of the Paradise made quick work of reminding Curtis that, despite his coup getting Jimmy and the Dreamettes on the stage of the Miami hotel's Crystal Room, his black ass was still in the Deep South. "Tell Jimmy and everybody else accompanying him to this evening's performance that they can use the dressing room, but they best eat and pee before they get here, 'cause ain't no darkies allowed in the dining rooms or the bathrooms," Martin Jack said simply from behind his office desk as a colored waiter, wearing white gloves and a bow tie and tails, placed his cocktail on a coaster before him. The waiter went about his business serving Martin Jack—a short, stubby man with a hairline that receded so far to the back of his head that, at the precise angle, he appeared to be bald—as if he were simply overhearing someone recite a recipe for sweet tea, but the word "darkie," and the ease with which Martin Jack said it, stung Curtis enough to make him flinch. He knew coming into this gig, though, that he had to develop skin as thick as buck hide to get what he came for: an audience with an *American Bandstand* producer, on his turf—with a roomful of white couples swaying to Jimmy's music. If the girls had to eat and use the bathroom at the host house over on Ellery Street for that to happen, and he had to endure a few "darkie" comments, so be it. Dick Clark, after all, was worth that much.

"No problem," Curtis said to Martin Jack, who'd already turned his attention to a magazine on his desk, making it clear he was finished with that particular conversation. Curtis took his cue and started to leave, hesitating if only for a moment as the waiter quickly jumped in front of the door and courteously opened it for him. "You have a good show now, Mr. Taylor, you hear?" he said, startling

Curtis, who hadn't expected the waiter to know who he was. Curtis simply nodded, and moved past. It was seven P.M. Jimmy and the girls would be there in half an hour, and he needed to be out back to greet the bus and make sure that everyone understood the ramifications of cutting up.

Twenty minutes later, though, the group made it clear that, despite the miracle Curtis had pulled off to get them onto that stage, Jimmy, Effie, and Deena weren't exactly interested in quelling his nerves with gratitude. Indeed, they unleashed a rolling cloud of drama as they tumbled down the bus steps. "I'm just saying, man, my audience ain't used to seeing me like *this*," Jimmy said, pointing at his hair, which had been conked and coiffed into a Perry Como helmet, much the opposite of his usual stand-at-attention hairdo that his stylist kept in place with a considerable amount of teasing and hair grease. "And what's with the suit, brother? Cream, jack? And my ladies? They look like bridesmaids at a white folks' wedding."

"Amen to that," Effie said as she grunted down the steps, the pointy heels, a size nine, squeezing the blood out of her size ten feet.

"I don't see anything wrong with these dresses," Deena chimed, patting her bouffant wig as she gazed at herself in a compact mirror. "I think they're rather nice."

"I think they're rather nice," Effie mocked. "Nice for a skinny minnie like yourself. Now a woman like me? It's a whole lot to be squeezing into this tight-ass bodice, I'll tell you that much. And all this damn crinoline in the skirt is making me itch something fierce. Lord ha' mercy, Curtis, you couldn't do better than this?"

Curtis, unmoved, didn't bother responding—just led the group in through the back door, down a small hallway, and past the kitchen, toward the dressing rooms. "Just stand here and wait—you'll be on in about fifteen minutes."

Just then, a waiter timidly walked up to Jimmy, shooed on by a few of his fellow workers, who'd been mumbling and watching the entourage from the time it hit the door. " 'Scuse me, suh," the waiter said to Jimmy. "My name is Cletus—Cletus Wilks. I stay over there by Miss Barbara, where y'all been taking up since you got to Miami. I just want to say it's a honor to see you here, and I—I mean we," he said, glancing back at his colleagues, who, along with all the other waiters and workers, stopped what they were doing to listen in, "we sure is happy to get y'all whatever y'all need. Don't too many colored folks come through here lessen they workin' the kitchen or cleanin' the rooms. It's gonna be right nice to see y'all up there on that stage. We all real proud of y'all. Right proud."

For the first time since he'd climbed into his Perry Como costume, Jimmy smiled. "Thank you, youngblood," he said, extending his hand, which Cletus eagerly reached for and shook with a firm grip. "You can help us out a lot if you pack up some of them steaks for us to carry outta here when we finished," he laughed.

"I know that's right," C.C. said.

Curtis, annoyed by the exchange but not so insensitive that he'd bust it up, excused himself. "I'll be in the back with the producer," he said simply as he straightened his tie and strolled away. "Get you head in the game and get ready," he called back over his shoulder. "This is it." Then to C.C., he said, "Let's go."

He might have looked unaffected when he reached the Crystal Room, but make no mistake about it: By the time he exchanged pleasantries with Mike Iger, the young, cocky *American Bandstand* producer, and took his seat in the shadows of the massive curtains flanking the side wall in the crowded theatre, Curtis was damn near faint. The evening, he thought, had to be perfect, and, after witnessing the show back on the bus and in the kitchen, he wasn't quite convinced Jimmy was ready to pull off his romp onto the white charts. But he knew he had to make this evening work. Had to. Curtis shook Mike's hand, introduced him to C.C., and offered him a cigar as he began trying to chat him up, but Mike wouldn't hear of it. He was too busy laughing at the house announcer, Sandy Price, an insult comic who was slashing and burning his way across the ballroom.

"Cuban? You're kidding, right?" Sandy said to a patron dressed in a tuxedo, a cigar dangling between his fingers. "I'm a Jew and you're a Cuban. I say this from the bottom of my heart: A Negro can move into my neighborhood, you can't," he said as the laughs quickly rippled across the largely liquor-hazed crowd. As if the laughter gave him a booster shot of energy, Price prowled toward his next victim, a chubby, overdressed woman sitting next to the Cuban. "You gotta be a Jew, lady—it's 105 degrees in here and you're the only one with a mink stole. Are you on vacation? And you're sitting next to the Cuban? You've taken your shots?"

Mike practically fell out of his chair. Curtis let out a nervous laugh, mostly to demonstrate to Mike that he was listening and enjoying the show, even though, clearly, he wasn't. The comic moved on to yet another man, this one an older gentleman sitting alone. "Oh my God, look at you. Anyone else hurt in the accident," Sandy said, eliciting even more laughter from the audience.

"No, sir," the older man said, trying to be a good sport.

"Don't call me sir," Sandy deadpanned. "You're not a Negro."

C.C. turned his whole body toward Curtis, with a what-the-hell-was-that? look on his face, but Curtis didn't give him anything back—just pasted a smile on his face and stared in the general direction of the comedian. C.C. watched as the service staff, mostly Cuban and black, moved quietly through the audience, seemingly not fazed by—and, most troubling to C.C., used to—the searing words flowing from the stage. Still, Curtis kept on his poker face.

"But really folks, God put us on this earth to laugh. We're all human beings. Jew, Gentile, Cuban, Negro, even Puerto Rican. Well, maybe not Puerto Rican," he said, the crowd laughing so hard it could hardly hear what he said next. "But tonight, we're about to make history. The first Negro headliners ever to play Miami Beach. Actually, it's a very convenient arrangement; these people can sing and dance *and* mop up afterward. You just can't get help like that anymore!"

Jimmy simply looked down and hung his head in defeat. Effie and Lorrell tossed each other a look, their eyes wide, their mouths open, so insulted by what they were hearing. As they stood on the stage waiting for the curtains to open, they didn't quite know whether to run off it or stand there so they could cuss out the little man in front of the white audience and stomp off in the most dramatic fashion. They both looked at Deena, who was smoothing out her skirt and squaring her shoulders, clearly removed from the insults. Indeed, she wasn't paying the M.C.'s jokes any mind—what else could anyone possibly expect in a place like the Paradise, where black help couldn't even put their black feet in the pool water to clean it, much less enjoy a swim? Deena's skin was much too thick to get all worked up over such things. She'd decided the moment they hit Miami's shores that she was there for one reason, and one reason only: to sing. She smiled her widest smile, struck her pose, and waited for the M.C. to continue.

"So please join me in welcoming the very talented Jimmy Early and the Dreamettes!" Sandy yelled into the microphone as the curtains pushed away to reveal Jimmy and the Dreamettes standing in silhouette.

As the band slogged its way through a watered-down version of "I Want You Baby," with Jimmy doing smoothed-out moves in front of the swaying Dreamettes, Curtis's eyes searched the room. He motioned for C.C. to look around: At the next table a young white couple was kissing.

Other couples were holding hands to the romantic music. Even the *American Bandstand* producer seemed mesmerized by the melodic rendition of the group's number one pop tune; he scribbled notes on a small pad, the words of which Curtis, try as he might, couldn't see.

Curtis took his shot. "Of course, we can put together a much younger look for *American Bandstand,*" he said to the producer, who offered up a noncommittal smile, then turned his attention back to the stage, just in time to witness Jimmy dropping his mellow act and launching into a soul riff. He drove it home with some pelvic thrusts and a *"Oooohhh—you got me beggin'/Oh baby baby baby baby please/Ooooh Ooooh!"* It was a signature riff that would have had women—sistahs—anywhere within a ten-block radius snatching their panties from up under their dresses and slamming them onto the stage, but not there at the Crystal Room. No, the reaction to Jimmy's sexually charged performance was received much differently; a white woman turned away, clearly rattled. Her husband grabbed her hand, and the two of them stood up noisily and stomped out of the ballroom. A few more couples walked out behind them as Jimmy, who had his eyes closed and was oblivious to the commotion he was stirring up, kept on riffing.

Curtis signaled to Lorrell, who tried to get

Jimmy's attention, but the damage was done; the *American Bandstand* producer flipped his pad closed and shut down any thoughts of Jimmy Early and the Dreamettes doing anything with Dick Clark that didn't involve shining his shoes. Curtis downed his drink and averted his eyes from Jimmy to Deena, who, unlike Lorrell and Effie, was keeping her cool through all the distractions. He looked around the room some more and noticed that other men in the audience—white men—were staring at Deena, too. Curtis lifted his finger in the air, signaling a waiter to his table. "A Scotch," he said, his eyes still on Deena. "Make that a double."

After the show, Lorrell, Deena, and Effie settled in front of the mirror in the dressing room and simultaneously pulled off their wigs.

"I love me some Jimmy, but he's gonna have to stop calling me baby," Lorrell said out of nowhere. "I'm a woman now," she said, staring intently into the mirror.

"Did you see that man Curtis was sitting with," Deena said excitedly, ignoring Lorrell.

"Did you hear what I said, Deena?" Lorrell said, turning to Deena. "I am a woman now."

"Lorrell, I know," Deena said, exasperated.

"What do you mean, you know? Has Jimmy talked?"

"He didn't have to," Deena said, disgust ringing in her words. "How could you, Lorrell? You're just a baby!"

"I am not, Deena! I'm a woman now," she yelled before catching herself. No need to involve the entire house in the conversation, she quickly surmised, lowering her voice. "I'm eighteen, so I'm a woman."

"Yeah, she's a mature woman like me," Effie said, picking imaginary lint out of her wig. "And she loves Jimmy just as much as I love Curtis. It's not wrong if you love someone."

Deena pushed herself from the vanity and pushed away from the girls. "Is that all you two can think about?" she asked.

"Yeah," Effie and Lorrell said together.

"There's no doubt that my mother brought me up better." Deena sighed.

"Oh Deena, you're just jealous," Lorrell said.

"Yeah, let yourself go—just once," Effie said. "It is so wonderful to have somebody to love," she said, touching her eyes in the mirror. She was startled when the door opened, but relaxed when she saw C.C.'s head poking through.

"You ladies decent?" he asked innocently.

"Well I am," Deena said. "I can't speak for these two."

Effie tossed an evil look in Deena's direction

that could have easily bored a hole through her skinny frame. C.C., followed by Curtis, walked in, oblivious to what Deena meant.

"So, Curtis, how'd it go with *American Bandstand*?" Deena gushed.

"Timing's not right," Curtis blurted.

"Well, maybe they'll be more interested after we play the Copa," Effie said.

"Y'all ain't playin' the Copa," Curtis said. His temple bounced as he rubbed his teeth together, a nervous tic that, of late, had become more intense. He hadn't intended on telling them the news like this, but he needed to play his hand quick if his plan was going to work. See, after his evening with Effie, Curtis had gone back to the Crystal Room and talked his way into a casual drink with the manager, who had been hanging around the bar area, alternately sloshing back shots of vodka and dirty martinis while he barked orders at the wait staff that was preparing the room for the next night's show. Curtis knew he needed to set things straight with ol' Martin Jack because he called the shots for one of the biggest stages in the country. It would take Martin Jack all of a phone call or two to spread the word to the Copa and all the other big whites-only clubs that Jimmy was cooning on the stage, scaring off all the good white women in the audience—and once that happened, Curtis and his musical acts would get a life sentence on the chitlin' circuit, never to be seen by white audiences or heard on the white radio stations again. This was not an option for Curtis. He took a sip of his Grand Marnier and got busy.

"So, there were a few kinks in the show, but it was still a good one, I think," Curtis said, rubbing his finger around the rim of his glass.

"You think so, huh?" Martin Jack asked. "Well, from my table, it looked like the kinks were a big problem. All that hip swizzlin'. This is a classy establishment with classy people who don't take kindly to that kind of performance—your peoples' kind of performance. I figure I lost a couple hundred bucks when those three tables left outta here, which means your kinks cost *me* cash."

"But if only three out of a hundred couples walked away, you still win . . . ?"

"You got that couple hundred to give me, boy? Reach in your pocket and pull that cash out, then tell me again that somebody's winning, even when they're losing money. That there kinda logic don't even make a bit of sense," Martin Jack said, downing another shot. "I tell you, the one thing that saved your ass tonight was that fox up there on the stage. That's a pretty little colored gal."

"Who you talking about?"

"The one with them great big ol' eyes," Martin Jack said, smiling.

"You mean Deena?"

"I don't know what her name is, all I know is she's a stallion."

Instantly, Curtis knew exactly what he needed to take his record label into another direction: Deena. She was pretty in a way that appealed to white men—skinny, affable, sexy even. He, too, saw the way the men were looking at her—the way their women squirmed in their seats when they realized their men were turned on by Deena's charm and class. And her voice, though weaker than Effie's down-home driver, was ideal for radio—much less identifiable, easier to swallow. Perfect for pop. She certainly had the class and grace to pull off the lead, unlike Effie, whose ego, Curtis imagined, would only balloon and fester into something wholly unmanageable.

By the time he got up from that bar with Martin Jack, Curtis knew what he had to do to keep Rainbow Records, and his dream to take over the pop charts, in play. He just needed to sell it to the girls. Or, more specifically, Effie.

"What you mean we ain't playing the Copa," Effie said, embarrassed that Curtis was going back on the pillow-talk tidbit he'd dropped just the night before. "You said—"

"I'm breaking you and Jimmy up," Curtis interrupted her. Lorrell swirled around like the devil himself was possessing her soul, and let Curtis have it.

"I know what you're doing, Curtis! You're breaking us up because you don't like me with Jimmy! None of you do because you're all jealous," she said, through her tears. "Well, nothing's breaking me and Jimmy up! Nothing!"

Curtis was a little taken aback by her hysteria—he knew Lorrell and Jimmy had slept together (Jimmy was damn near ready to hang a sign from the back window of the bus letting everyone know he'd popped her cherry), but he didn't expect that Lorrell would have a problem stepping out of Jimmy's shadow. He knew shutting her down wasn't going to be the problem. Effie, on the other hand . . .

"I'm breaking you up because Jimmy's going back on the road while you stay here to open your own act," Curtis said quietly.

All three of the women stopped in their tracks, stunned.

"Did you say our own act?" Deena asked, her eyes as wide as saucers.

"Finally," Effie boomed. "This is what I've been waiting for. Curtis I love you!" she said, throwing her arms around his neck.

And just as quickly as Lorrell's waterworks turned on, they shut down. "Honey, I'm fine with that," she said, just as cool as you please. "I love me some Jimmy, but I don't want to be singing behind him the rest of my life!"

Curtis stood and moved to the center of the dressing room. "Ladies and gentlemen—presenting the Dreams!" The girls giggled and clapped as Curtis extended his arms out wide and smiled. " 'Dreamettes' are little girls. You're women now."

"See, Deena? I told you." Lorrell laughed, though Deena didn't acknowledge the joke.

"We're opening in a week at the Crystal, so there's gonna be a lot of work and a lot of changes," Curtis continued. "I'm bringing in Jolly Jenkins to stage a whole new show. He's done movies, Broadway, club acts, you name it . . ."

"But C.C. does our steps." Effie frowned. "He's always done our steps."

"It's okay, Effie," C.C. said, making his presence felt for the first time since the news. Curtis had already told C.C. of his plans to hire a new choreographer—did a good job, too, of selling his young charge on the merits of hiring someone to "get the girls dancing while you focus on the music." C.C. started to put up a fuss—he'd always been able to handle the writing and the dancing. But Curtis shut him down quickly: "Listen man, you're a good songwriter, but you have the potential to be a great songwriter, and that ain't gonna happen if you standing on the stage trying to tell the girls how to move their hips. Now let me handle the business and you stick to the music," Curtis said firmly. C.C. was none too pleased, but once he cooled down and thought about what Curtis said, he understood it and, as always, did as Curtis said.

"Jolly's the best there is," C.C. said simply.

Curtis walked over and stood in front of Deena, a smile still plastered across his dark, expansive face. "We'll have new wigs, the most expensive. And brand-new costumes, ones that'll appeal to a younger crowd," he said, making her giggle. Curtis was looking into Deena's eyes when he dropped the bomb. "And Effie—Deena's going to sing lead."

"Deena's doing what?!" Effie said, spinning around to look Curtis in the face.

"Lead," he said simply.

"What do you mean? I always sing lead," she said, shifting from one foot to the other, her hands resting on her hips. "Tell him, C.C."

"We're trying something new, Effie," C.C. said quietly, his betrayal evident in his voice.

"You knew about this?" Effie asked quietly, confused and hurt.

"Curtis and I talked it over just now," C.C. said. "He says it's only temporary."

Effie paced the room, her words gushing as quickly as her thoughts would allow. "We finally get the chance to have our own act and Deena's doing lead? She can't sing like I can," Effie boomed.

"She's right, Curtis—I can't," Deena agreed, her face falling. She'd always admired Effie's ability to belt out a note, and understood from jump that her voice was a great complement to Effie's special instrument—certainly not the one that would stir an audience to its feet. She wanted nothing more than to be a star, but she wasn't so sure she could carry the stage like Effie could, or stir the audience into a frenzy like the rest of the day's soul singers. "I don't want to do it."

"You'll do what I tell you," Curtis snapped. "This is a new sound, with a new look . . ."

"A new look?" Effie said, reeling back. "Nobody can see her on a record!"

Curtis was growing impatient; he couldn't understand why they couldn't see the vision he had of making the Dreams into a world-class act. "The only way we're going to change things is by appealing to kids. And kids today are watching television." Curtis knew what he'd just said was cold, but it was what it was.

"So Deena's going to sing lead because you like

the way she looks?" Effie said quietly, tears welling in her eyes. "Am I ugly to you, Curtis?"

"Of course not, baby," he said, rushing over to Effie and stroking her face. "You know how I feel about you. Don't make this personal."

"Well, what am I supposed to do? Deena's beautiful. She's always been beautiful, but I've got the voice, Curtis. I've got the voice. You can't put me in back. You just can't."

"Effie, you'll be singing backup with me," Lorrell interjected, trying to comfort Effie. "What's so wrong with that? Shoot, let Deena do all the work for a change."

C.C., who had been told of the changes shortly before the girls were told, had the same reaction as his sister at first. Having Effie lead the Dreamettes to chart-topping success, after all, was what the two had imagined for themselves, and was all the two had ever poured all their hearts and souls into. And just as their dream was about to be realized, there was Curtis, editing the picture with unfathomable changes that would give Effie nothing more than a supporting role. "You can't do this to my sister," C.C. had told Curtis earlier. "It'll kill her."

"That's why I'm coming to you to ease her into this thing, youngblood," Curtis said. "Now hear me out, son—you got to work with me on this thing. We are about to take the music world by storm, you and I, and if we're going to do all the things that we planned, we have to do it right—don't you agree?"

"Well, yeah, but . . ."

"But nothing, youngblood," Curtis said, cutting him off. "You got to realize, I haven't led you wrong yet, and I'm not about to start doing that now. Does your sister have talent? Yes. Can she sing better than most of these R&B singers on the charts? Hell yes. Can you get the Dreams onto the pop charts? Hell no. Not with her sound, not with her look. But we can certainly make them come around to her as a lead singer once we get there. And we get there with Deena. Just trust me on this. You got to talk to her—you got to make her understand this when I announce the changes, or otherwise, there won't be no Dreams, there won't be no pop charts, there won't be no Rainbow Records, there won't be no you and me. Just give me some time, brother. Handle your sister."

And C.C. did, because despite the foulness of it all, he knew Curtis was right. C.C. had bought into Curtis's dream of mainstreaming the Dreamettes, and now that they were on the cusp of making it happen, he couldn't half-step now. And so he did as Curtis told him, and went to work on

Effie. "Your voice alone is too special," he reasoned. "We need a lighter sound to cross over to the pop charts. It's what we need."

"What about what I need?" Effie huffed.

It's more than you
It is more than me
No matter what we are
We are a family
This dream is for all of us
This one can be real
And you can't stop us now
Because of how you feel

Curtis, Deena, and Lorrell joined Effie and C.C. on the stage. C.C. pressed on.

It's more than you
It is more than me
Whatever dreams we have
They're for the family
We're not alone anymore
Now there are others there
And that dream's big enough
For all of us to share
So don't think you're going
You're not going anywhere
You're staying

And taking your share
And if you get afraid again
I'll be there

Deena and Lorrell stepped up to Effie, and joined Curtis.

We are a family
Like a giant tree
Branching out toward the sky
We are a family
We are so much more
Than just you and I
We are a family
Like a giant tree
Growing stronger
Growing wiser
We are growing free
We need you
We are family

Effie couldn't believe what she was hearing—couldn't fathom the implications behind it. But she knew that if Curtis, her man, had convinced her biggest fan—her little brother—that this was for the best, then she really had no other choice but to go along with it. The battle had already been fought and won, and she had to concede. Defeated, Effie fell into Curtis's arms and buried her head in his shoulder. Her man and her flesh and blood had made a decision. Clearly, there was nothing she could do about it—but accept.

"I'm amazed, Mr. Taylor. Much as I love my daughter, I've never thought she had much of a voice," said May Jones as her finger followed the trail of a bead of water dripping down her glass of club soda. She could hardly take her eyes off Deena, up on the stage, center mic, dressed in a sophisticated white gown, beckoning to the men in the Crystal Room's audience. It seemed that just last week, she had been holed up in their tiny apartment, dressed in bobby socks and oversized skirts and ill-fitting sweaters, her nose in schoolbooks. What could her shy, soft-spoken bookworm of a 19-year-old daughter possibly know about what a man's "special dream" is? But there Deena was, looking every bit as sexy and sophisticated as any female star May had ever seen (not that that was many; May much preferred the gospel stylings of the Caravans to the sexually suggestive lyrics and dance moves that came with secular music). So taken aback by Deena's new mature look was May when she saw her child in the dressing room just before the show that her first inclination was to haul her behind back to Detroit, where Deena could forget all this nonsense about being a singer and get back into her books so she could become something respectable—admirable—like a nurse, or a teacher, like her mama, and her mama before that. That, after all, was what May had worked so hard for all those years, struggling to teach the kids at the local colored school. May, you see, didn't believe in all that get-rich-and-travel-the-world talk Effie and Lorrell had been feeding her daughter; that kind of success didn't come to Negroes often, and when it did, they got caught up in so much mess, what with the drugs and the alcohol and the sex and whatnot, that just as quickly as they reached that high, they came tumbling down, hard.

Which was why May was hardly impressed when Curtis sent for her so she could witness her daughter's debut as the lead singer in the Dreams. Actually, she told Curtis she wasn't interested in seeing the show, and was half a step from ordering her child back to Detroit for a "proper education" when Curtis turned on the charm and convinced her that Deena's transformation was something she needed to see for herself. And when Deena burst onto the stage in a stream of glittering light and May got a gander of her daughter's voice lifted up by the twelve-piece band and the strength of Effie and Lorrell's voices, even May got lured into the seductive aura of Deena's rising stardom. Shoot, May was gripping that glass to keep herself from snapping her fingers to the scandalous words Deena cooed from the stage: *"We're your dream girls/Boys we'll make you happy, yeah!/We're your dream girls/Boys we'll always care/We're your dream girls, dream girls will never leave you/No no, and all you got to do is dream, baby/We'll be there."* The girls pointed at the crowd, and then opened their hands in a come-hither gesture. May was mesmerized.

"Deena's got something better—a quality," Curtis said, leaning into May as she watched her daughter.

"You make her sound like a product," May said, Curtis's voice snapping her out of her gaze.

Curtis considered what she said, and broke out into a grin. "A product. I like that."

Products, you see, can be packaged, sold, and consumed by most anyone, if you know the market and how to work it. And Curtis knew from watching Deena up on that stage—and the audience that was drinking her in—that with the right marketing strategy, his "product" could be bigger than any stage show at the Crystal Room. Much bigger. And so from then on, Curtis focused exclusively on making sure Deena had every tool available to her to become the lead singer he needed her to be—the right dresses, a phalanx of makeup artists, seamstresses, hairstylists, and comportment experts dedicated to giving her the right "look" she needed and teaching her to command the stage and the media like the best of them. Needless to say, Deena hadn't a problem stepping into the role. By the time the group's single "Dreamgirls" hit number one on the pop charts—just a month and a half after the trio was introduced on the Crystal Room stage—Deena was smelling herself, for real. The devil reared her ugly head one day at Rainbow Records, where the press had been invited for a photo op of the Dreams as they accepted their first gold record.

"Curtis," Deena said, breezing into his office unannounced. "Sweetie, this gown just will not do. The color is all wrong and the seamstresses poked me with the needle while they were stitching the bodice. I just can't have this happen on such an important day. Can't you do something?"

She didn't notice Effie, having been turned down yet again for the lead vocal on the Dreams' next single, sulking in the corner chair behind the door. Effie couldn't believe she was standing in her man's office, talking to him like he was the help, complaining that the dress she insisted the group wear wasn't good enough. And where in the hell did she get off calling him "sweetie"? Effie had to mentally will herself not to jump up out of her chair.

It was only after Deena read the plastered smile on Curtis's face and followed his eyes to Effie's chair that she realized they weren't alone. "Oh, Effie, hi," she said dismissively, then turned back to Curtis. "So, what are we going to do about this?"

"We aren't going to do anything about it," Effie huffed. "You picked the dress knowing full well it wouldn't fit but one of us the right way—the skinniest one. Now you wear it or go out there naked."

"Excuse me?" Deena said, reeling back. "What on earth are you talking about? I do not recall asking you for your opinion . . ."

"Ladies, ladies," Curtis said, standing up from his chair and raising his hands to signal the women to stop the fighting. "We have exactly a half hour until the TV crews show up; there's no time to change the wardrobe now." He walked over to Deena and looked her in her eyes: "You look absolutely stunning in that dress, and you will wow them this afternoon. Now go and sit and relax and wait for your fans. Today is going to be a magnificent day, baby."

Effie, disgusted by the entire affair, rushed out of the room. It was Lorrell who convinced her that it wouldn't be a good idea to skip the press conference, a decision buoyed the moment Effie walked out into the showroom and saw all the fans pressed up against the window trying to get a better view of the Dreams. But Effie's euphoria plunged again when the reporters started lobbing their questions at Curtis, and he obliged them in a way Effie never expected.

"People ask me how I came up with this sound, and I always tell 'em it's like makin' a great sundae," Curtis gushed in front of the cameras. "You start with a scoop of ice cream, then you sweeten it with some chocolate sauce, nuts, and a great big cherry on top."

"And is Deena the cherry?" a reporter yelled.

"Miss Jones is the cherry, the whipped cream, the sauce, the nuts, and the banana, too!" And with that, the reporters rushed Deena, pushing Effie back as if she weren't even there.

For sure, they weren't the only ones pushing her back. Curtis had even moved his campaign to make Effie irrelevant into their bedroom—had taken to frequent "business trips" that had him disappearing for days on end, sometimes staying holed up in a hotel room in the city when he was too tired to drive back to his apartment. When he was around, he was too busy in the studio or going down to the local clubs and radio stations to push the group's latest single to pay Effie any mind, and even when she dressed up in her finest negligees and bathed herself in her sweetest perfumes and left her hair untied and wore her lipstick to bed, he turned her away.

"Come on and save your mama's soul, 'cause I need a little sugar in my bowl," she sang softly in his ear when he crawled into his bed on a rare early night. She'd overheard him turning down C.C.'s invitation to watch him sit in with the band at a small after-hours club over on Twelfth Street—something about how he wanted to stay in and get some shut-eye so he could be in the studio early—so she rushed upstairs, got extra pretty, and lay in wait for him in his bedroom.

Curtis gave Effie a peck on her cheek and turned over, his back building a massive wall to stave off her sexual advances. Undaunted, Effie pushed her body up close to his back, her breasts falling softly against his shoulder blades. She reached around his body and slowly rubbed Curtis's chest and stomach, and then massaged her way farther down his lower torso. "Come on baby, put a little sugar in my bowl," she cooed.

Curtis let out a heavy sigh, reached down, and pushed Effie's hand away. "Effie, not now—really . . ."

"If not now, when, Curtis? Because my sugar bowl is damn near empty," Effie huffed, pulling back from his body. "What's the problem, huh? Tell me something."

"There is no problem—I'm just tired is all," he said simply. "Now if you don't mind, I need to get some rest, and I suggest you do, too, seeing as you gotta be up just as early as me to do that radio show and then rehearse so we can cut that record tomorrow night. Can you shut off my light please?"

Effie fought back the tears as she got up and opened the bedroom door. She gave her man one last look before she pulled the light switch and quietly walked out, shutting the door behind her without another word. She went toward the kitchen, and enveloped her sadness in a bowl of butter pecan and praline ice cream, then sat, seething, on the living room couch well into the night.

C.C. rushed in a little after four A.M., terror in his eyes. "Effie, the police and all them colored folks down there at Etta's Joint done lost they mind," he said, practically tearing off his coat as he paced the floor.

Effie, woozy from sleep deprivation and anger, was in no mood for C.C.'s theatrics. "Boy, what the hell you talkin' about? It's damn near four in the morning—comin' in here yellin' like you ain't got the sense of a billy goat."

"I'm tellin' you Effie, something's going down over there on Twelfth Street. I ain't never seen nothin' like this. I think the brothers done caught a touch of that Watts riot fever over there."

"What you talking about?" Effie asked, still confused.

"Well, the police ran up in there just after our last set, talkin' about they was shuttin' the place down and everything, and when they loaded up some people into the paddy wagon, somebody threw a bottle and a couple cans at the police, and damn you would have thought somebody threw a lit match at a gas pump because it got hot down there real quick, Effie. They down there rioting."

"What?" Effie asked, finally understanding the urgency of Curtis's words. She sat up. "You didn't get caught up in that mess did you?"

"Oh hell no—Curtis would skin my ass alive if he knew I was down there in the middle of that," C.C. said. He sat down on the couch and took off his shoes. "I'll tell you, though, there was something different about what was going on down there. Brothers are fed up, and I can't say I blame them."

C.C. made the mistake of saying that out loud in front of Curtis later that evening, while they were taking a break between takes of the Dreams' song "Heavy," a single that was going onto their new album. Wayne was fiddling with the speakers and some of the other equipment, and Deena and Lorrell were joking with the band, while Curtis was stirring through some paperwork he was reading for a big artist signing he had coming up the day after. The TV set played silently in the corner, near where Effie was sulking; they all could hear sirens and gunfire just outside the door.

"Boy what you talking about?" Curtis asked.

"I'm—I'm just saying, Curtis, I think people have a right to stand up for themselves, especially when the man keep putting his foot on they neck," C.C. said. The noise of broken glass outside made him flinch.

Curtis placed his pen down, and sat back in his chair. "Tell me, C.C., how are you standing up for yourself when you're burning down your own house? Tell me that."

"I just . . . was . . . sayin' . . ."

"You're right: What's going on out there is important. But it ain't got nothing to do with what we're doing here. You got your fancy car, your pretty house, and your pretty clothes, and all of that comes from working hard and making hits. Now why don't you have a seat and write some more music. That's what's going to help a brother out."

"But see that's just it," C.C. said. "People out in the streets are starting to question why we sit in this building making records and putting on our fancy clothes and doing press appearances and singing for all-white audiences at all-white hotels while our hometown is burning. How can we be the sound of the youth when the youth are up in arms, screaming for help? How can we ignore it?"

"We ain't ignoring," Curtis said simply. "We making music. And every dime that comes up in here goes into the pockets of *the brothers*, you dig? We support the NAACP. I recorded Martin Luther King, didn't I? That's more than enough commitment to the cause. Now we all best get back to work, or else all of us are gonna be out there on that street."

C.C., defeated, sat down; everyone in the room was looking everywhere but at him. C.C. understood—shoot, admired—Curtis's work ethic. But he couldn't quite reconcile how his boss could be so apolitical when it came to what was going on in the streets. Weren't they, after all, depending on those very people to buy the records they were making? Somehow, some way, C.C. decided, he was going to do more—needed to. But Curtis was right: If they didn't make music, none of them was going to get paid—and if none of them got paid, no one was going to eat. And that certainly wasn't going to help anybody's cause.

Sirens pierced the silence. Curtis pushed his paperwork to the side. "Wayne, you ready?"

"Yup. Ready boss."

"Let's go then," Curtis said, his words making everyone rush back to his position in the studio—everyone save Effie, who casually sauntered to her microphone without much pep in her step. She rolled her eyes at Curtis, but he didn't notice.

"Record 'Heavy, Heavy.' Take thirty," Wayne said into the intercom.

The music started up, and Deena leaned into the microphone, her eyes closed. She began to sing: *"You used to be so light and free/You used to smile just looking at me/Now all you give is jealous hate/Come on, baby, better lose some weight."*

Effie and Lorrell chimed in, *"Heavy, heavy/You got so heavy, baby/Heavy, heavy/You got so heavy on me."*

Curtis punched the intercom button with his

fist. "Stop!" He jumped up and moved into the recording booth. "Effie, you're still too loud," he seethed, continuing his night-long battle to get Effie to tone down her soulful voice, which was overpowering Deena's more subdued lead.

"I'm trying, Curtis—" Effie started.

"If you won't ease up, I'll do it for you," Curtis spat, repositioning Effie's mike away from her face. "Now get it right."

Effie bit her lip, humiliated.

"Maybe we should come back in the morning," Deena said softly.

Curtis eased up his tone a bit. "This album's a month late already," he said. "Look, I know you're tired. But it's the last cut."

Deena smiled, if only a little, a gesture that looked even tender. Effie noticed it, her eyes going back and forth between Deena's and Curtis's. It wasn't until that exact moment that she realized it, but now she knew something was up.

"Let's go again," Curtis said, averting his gaze from Effie's.

But it was too late; when the girls started singing again, Effie purposefully sang her part with a strong, in-the-midnight-hour alto that completely overpowered Deena's voice. Deena and Lorrell stopped singing and looked at Effie like she'd lost her mind. Effie kept going, though, pulling the microphone closer to her and holding the last note, aimed directly at Curtis. *"Me!"* And then she stormed toward the door.

"Where do you think you're going?" Curtis yelled, pushing his chair back from the mixing board.

"Curtis, you're a liar!" Effie yelled.

"Now you watch it, Effie!"

"You're sleeping with her. And everyone knows it!" she said, pushing open the door through the lobby and to the front door. She stepped outside into the night air, which was thick with soot and smoke. In the distance an entire city block was on fire. Young colored folks, their Afros bouncing, seemed to be dancing in the flames, their fists raised, their screams a rallying cry.

"Effie, get back in here!" Curtis shouted, just as a car screeched toward them. The driver took random potshots with a handgun. Curtis grabbed Effie and pulled her back in. "Black-owned business! We're black-owned!" Curtis yelled, taking cover.

The driver retreated. "Black power, brother!" he yelled as he sped off to his next pursuit, shooting bullets into the air. As Curtis made his way back into the storefront, Effie collapsed into his arms.

"I don't feel well, Curtis," she said.

He just looked at her as they headed back into the recording studio; neither said another word.

Deena, Effie, and Lorrell emerged onto the stage of CBS's *Star Cavalcade,* a wave of dry ice parting to reveal the three stunning women, dressed in tight orange dresses. Deena moved center stage and sang into the camera like it was a lover. In the control room, Curtis was barking orders at the technical director.

"Tighten up on camera two," he said.

Irritated, the TV director complied. "Move in camera two," he said.

Effie swayed left and tried to catch the attention of the camera, so she, too, could sing directly to the audience. But, what do you know? Every last camera was focused on Deena.

"Unbelievable," Effie muttered.

It was Lorrell, whose job it was to stay in synch with Effie while Deena riffed, who first noticed her group mate rush from the stage. She chased after her, calling out "Effie!" Deena caught a gander of what was going on when she saw on the monitor she was the only one standing on the stage. Terrified, she rushed off, too.

"Effie, you're going crazy!" Lorrell yelled as she chased Effie down the backstage corridor. Effie turned around and stared a hot hole into Deena, who was bringing up the rear.

"Tell me what I've done!" Deena said, though she knew full well what the drama was all about.

"You stole my dream, Deena! And you stole my man!"

Curtis emerged from a stage door, furious. "I won't have this kind of talk anymore!" he yelled.

Effie ignored him. "Don't act like you don't know what this is about!" she yelled.

"Effie, stop screaming. Everybody can hear," Lorrell said.

"I don't care. Let 'em all hear!"

"I'm warning you, Effie," Curtis said through his teeth as he grabbed her arm. "Stop bringing us down."

"Why, Curtis? You don't need me. All you care about is her bony ass," Effie said.

Curtis lifted his hand and, for a moment, considered slapping her face. But he thought better of it. Instead, he pointed in her face. "Back. Off."

"Or what?" Effie said, staring him down, daring him to hit her—touch her, even.

Curtis's attention, though, had switched from Effie to the CBS bigwigs; he wasn't about to have the show's producers, who by now were all crowded into the hallway, taking in all the Negro drama. He was much more concerned about all the damage control he'd have to do to ease their minds over the failed performance, so it was important for him to deal with Effie with dignity, at least in front of them. So he said nothing to Effie.

"I didn't think so," Effie said, rushing out the back door and into the night. She emerged from the back alley of the CBS soundstage with mascara-laced tears streaking down her cheeks. The musty air made her stomach do a somersault. Effie tried to keep the nausea at bay, but it was too late; the vomit had already found its way to her throat, and past her tongue, against her teeth, and finally out of her mouth and onto the sidewalk, her shoes, her dress. She rushed into a nearby diner and asked the first waitress she saw for a napkin.

"Ain't you that colored girl in that group?" she inquired.

"Please, do you have a napkin I can use?" Effie practically begged.

The woman looked Effie up and down and said, "Sure. But you got to take it outside. We don't need no coloreds getting sick in here while our good patrons are trying to eat."

Effie snatched the napkin from the woman, wiped her mouth, squared her shoulders and walked, with all the dignity she could muster, back out the door. Her stomach roiled some more when she smelled the musty air again. She didn't want to believe it—could hardly bring herself to—but Effie knew she'd have to go see a doctor to confirm what she knew deep down in her soul to be true.

A few days later, while Effie was at the doctor's office listening to the nurse confirm that she was 3 months pregnant, Lorrell and Deena were onstage in Las Vegas, in the final technical rehearsal. "Ladies and gentlemen, the Showroom at Caesars Palace is proud to present the sensational Deena Jones and the Dreams!" the announcer said, Lorrell and Deena's cue to emerge through a tinsel curtain onto a vast stage, where a dozen slender mirrors surrounded them. There was an empty spot where Effie was supposed to be. Deena and Lorrell kept singing and running through the number like nothing was wrong. C.C. was giving notes to the band, with Curtis just beyond the wings, bossing the stagehands around.

Deena and Lorrell were in full costume by the time Effie did make her way to the ballroom; they were running through their opening number. "Sorry I'm late," Effie said as she pulled off her coat. Deena and Lorrell froze. The rehearsal pianist and drummer stopped playing—and C.C. moved toward the stage. It was about to be a showdown, and everybody who'd been reluctantly waiting for the drama knew it was about to be on.

C.C. thought he could cushion the blow. "Effie . . ." he started.

"C.C., sorry I missed rehearsals, but I went to the doctor and I'm feeling much better now," she said as she moved toward the stage.

"Look, don't try to make it tonight," he said.

"What are you talking about, baby? It's New Year's Eve."

C.C. hesitated some more. "Curtis just stepped out to make a call. Why don't you go up to your room and later he'll come up and talk to you."

"I said I'm fine," Effie said, frowning. She turned to Deena and Lorrell and knew by the looks on their faces, that something was up. "Excuse me, I have to go get dressed now."

Just as Effie was about to walk off, Michelle Morris, the company receptionist, walked through the tinsel curtain wearing Effie's costume, which had been cut down and pinned to her body. She was oblivious to the tension in the room, and most certainly didn't notice Effie. "Oh God, I'm so nervous. I think I've got the steps down, but these harmonies . . ." She stopped when she saw Effie.

By now, Effie's eyebrows were so furrowed you would have thought she was going to squeeze her own eyeballs out. "C.C., what's going on? Lorrell, what's going on?"

"Effie, Curtis was supposed to—"

"Love me," Effie said simply. "Curtis was supposed to love me."

Curtis, who had reentered the room, saw Effie and motioned for the band and technicians to take a break. "There you are, Effie," he breezed. "I've been looking all over—" He stopped speaking when he saw Michelle.

"I turn my back for one minute—go take care of some personal business, and you go and replace me in my own damn group? The group I created?" she fumed.

Curtis decided to drop the niceties. "I've been warning you for months to clean up your act. You've been mean, late, giving everybody trouble. And today you didn't even bother to show up for rehearsal."

"That's a lie—I'm not giving trouble. I was just at the doctor's office today—I wasn't feeling well."

"Effie please—it's not just about today. This has been going on way too long—the mean streak, the destructive behavior. And you're getting so fat you're throwing off the uniformity of the group. You need a break."

"What? I've never been thinner," Effie said, looking down at herself as if that would somehow prove her point. "You're just saying that because you've been knocking off a piece of her skinny, common ass."

"Who you calling common?" Deena asked, putting her hands on her hips. "You know what? You're nothing but a self-indulgent, self-absorbed nonprofessional."

"You," Effie screamed back at her. "I'm calling you that common piece of ass he's knocking off."

"Now you listen to me, Miss Blame It on the World," Deena said through clenched teeth. "I've put up with you for much too long—all that bitching and nagging and screaming, too."

"Aaaah, hell," Lorrell chimed in. "When are you two gonna stop all this fighting?"

"Stay out of this, Lorrell. This is between Deena and me."

"Yeah?" Lorrell said, incredulous. "It's between me, too. I'm as much a part of this group as anybody else. And I'm tired, Effie. I'm tired of all the problems you're making for us!"

Effie shook her head furiously, as if somehow she could shake Lorrell's words out of her head and back out into the universe. She threw her hand in the air and pointed: "I always knew you two were ganging up on me!"

"She had nothing to do with this change," Deena said calmly. "It was you, always thinking of you."

Curtis hopped onto the stage and gripped Effie's shoulder to make his point. "I knew you were going to be trouble," he said.

"Trouble? Curtis, I'm your woman!"

"But you're getting out now. I'm not building this group to have you tear it apart. Go ahead and rant and scream and shout all you want to. I'm going to buy you out."

"There's no money dirty enough to buy me out! You remember that, Curtis," Effie yelled.

"Lay off, Effie—just take the money and run," C.C. said, his eyes betraying his weariness.

Effie swung around and stared her brother in the face. "You're in this with them, C.C.?"

"Cool it, Effie. This time you know what you've done," C.C. said.

"So they've bought your black ass, too, huh?"

"I said cool it, Effie—you've gone too far."

"Oh, I can go further—I can go further than this here," Effie said as she began pacing the stage.

Michelle wished she could melt into the wings—or go back and type up a memo or something. "I don't want to stay around this, y'all. I'm just breaking into this business. This is between all of you—this is none of my affair."

"Yeah, well it's between you, too, now, little sister. This snow job is as much your sin. How much did you put out to get in?"

"Now you watch your mouth, Ms. Effie White!" Michelle said, finding her voice. "I'm not about to take that from a second-rate diva who can't sustain."

"All right, everybody out. Me and Effie gotta talk," Curtis ordered, a stampede of bodies following the direction of his finger to the backstage. "Look, Effie, you dug your own grave on this one," he said after everyone was gone. "I mean, come on, we're at Caesars Palace, and you were nowhere to be found. What was I supposed to do?"

Effie didn't say another word, just stood there. But Curtis kept trying to reason with her. He didn't really care if she agreed to it or not—the show, as he created it, with Michelle replacing Effie, was going to go on exactly as planned. But he wanted to hear Effie acknowledge that she, not he, was the cause of the whole mess. "Maybe later on down the line, when you get your act together, we can reconsider putting you back in, but I just don't see that happening with this kind of behavior coming from you."

Effie simply closed her eyes, and started doing what she did best.

And I am telling you, I'm not going
You're the best man I'll ever know
There's no way I could ever go
No, no, there's no way
No no no no way
I'm living without you
I'm not living without you

I don't want to be free
I'm staying, I'm staying
And you, and you
You're gonna love me
You're gonna love me
And I am telling you, I'm not going
Even though the rough times are showing
There's just no way, There's no way
We're part of the same place
We're part of the same time
We both share the same blood
We both have the same mind
And time and time
We've had so much to share
I'm not waking up tomorrow morning
And finding that there's nobody there
Darling, There's no way
No, no, no, no way
I'm living without you
I'm not living without you, you see
There's no way, there's no way
Please don't go away from me
Stay with me, stay with me
Stay, stay, and hold me
Stay, stay, and hold me
Please stay and hold me, Mr. Man
Try it, mister, try it, mister
I know, I know you can

Tear down the mountains
Yell, scream and shout
You can say what you want
I'm not walking out
Stop all the rivers
Push strike and kill
I'm not gonna leave you
There's no way I will
And I am telling you, I'm not going
You're the best man I'll ever know
There's no way I could ever go
No no there's no way
No, no, no, no way
I'm living without you
I'm not living without you
Not living without you
I don't want to be free
I'm staying, I'm staying
And you, and you, and you
You're gonna love me . . .

Effie held her last, anguished, defiant note, and then opened her eyes to see that she was alone—Curtis was gone.

SIX

He had proposed to her in Paris, while they strolled alongside La Seine, gazing at the lights that twinkled on the edges of the Eiffel Tower. It was a rare moment of downtime, what with the concerts and the press conferences and the tours and the media-packed shopping expeditions. Deena was exhausted. She was, after all, the star of Deena Jones and the Dreams, and with that came the responsibility of being the one who did all the heavy lifting—leading all the songs on both record and stage, answering all the reporters' questions, being the perfect picture of poise around all the European delegates and government officials that insisted on holding court for her and the girls, dressing and looking the part at all hours of the day and night, lest some camera catch her looking less than impeccable. Deena wanted more than anything to be able to go out into the night air without a care in the world who saw her holding her man's hand, without having to put on a show pretending they weren't together—something they'd done from the moment Curtis seduced her in his glamorous hideaway bungalow in Michigan, way before Effie figured it all out. He'd said keeping their affair clandestine was necessary to keep the media—and everyone else, for that matter—focused on the prize: the Dreams becoming international celebrities, with as many fans and as much influence, money, and prestige as the Beatles. "You," Curtis would tell Deena, "are the black, female John Lennon. Without him, the Beatles don't exist. Same thing for our group—no Deena, no Dreams."

Deena was anxious to please Curtis, whose prestige and power she drank like a fine wine. She adored his strength—the way he commanded the room when he walked into it, the way everyone clung to his every word, anxious to do as he said, knowing that no matter how crazy it was, it was going to work because Curtis was a kingmaker, a man who could coax water out of a rock and turn it into the sweetest of elixirs. She'd watched with great admiration as he grew Rainbow Records into the label of choice for quality music, with star power unmatched by any of the other small-time record labels that struggled to put out a record or two before folding in a jumbled heap of financial ruin and career failures. While they all faltered, Curtis was busy building up his label with a roster of superstars—the Beat Machine, DeeDee Dawson, the Family Funk, Martha Reed, and a phenomenal band of kid brothers, the Campbell Connection. Under Curtis's direction, each one of those groups dominated the R&B and pop charts, with the Dreams as the centerpiece of all of Rainbow Records' jewels.

And just as powerful and decisive as he was in the boardroom, Curtis was sensitive in the bedroom—tender and gentle. He was Deena's first, and she would have had it no other way. She loved him deeply—unconditionally. And so Deena, in love and turned all the way out, followed Curtis's plan for her success to the letter, dressing the way he told her to, singing the way he told her to, and talking the way he told her to. But it wasn't as easy for either of them to hold back on the public displays of affection. She couldn't hide what she felt for him, and, strong as Curtis was, he couldn't either. Feelings, after all, don't—can't—lie. And nosy sisters are always going to find a way to tell *everybody* the truth. So between the tender looks Deena and Curtis exchanged, and the gossip Rhonda and Janice spread among the band players and everybody else with two ears and the ability to understand the words coming out of their mouths, most everybody knew that Deena and Curtis were a hot item.

Finally, after a short stint with public courting—Curtis started holding her hand and kissing her in front of the media when he realized their coupling could produce a storm of publicity for him and the Dreams—Curtis made it official: he asked Deena for her hand in marriage, and on that night, by the most beautiful river in Paris, she accepted without hesitation. "Yes, yes, yes—I'll marry you Curtis Taylor, Jr.," she squealed, jumping up and down as she wrapped her arms around his neck. They embraced and fell into a long, passionate kiss, and Deena just knew there was no other place she'd rather be. "We can buy us a beautiful home in the hills of Michigan, and have us a bunch of babies . . ."

"Whoa," Curtis said, gently pulling back from Deena's embrace. "Wait a minute, now, we gonna get hitched but we still got a lot of work to do. The Dreams are international now, and we can't stop that momentum for nine months while you carry a baby around . . ."

"But . . . don't you want a family with me?" she stammered.

"Of course, baby, you know I do," Curtis said,

easing his tone as he stroked her face. "I want to have babies with my wife—just not now. There will be plenty of time for us to make our family bigger, but right now, our baby is this group, our label, our dream of making Deena Jones and the Dreams the most successful pop group in history. We can't afford to lose sight of that now, baby. In a few years, we can think about it. Just not right now. You understand, baby, don't you?"

Deena was silent for a moment, but reluctantly shook her head yes.

"And, um, about the house in Michigan," he said, hesitating. "We can do that, but our main residence will have to be close to the offices of Rainbow Records, and I've decided that we need to take the label in a new direction. We're going west, baby. We're moving to L.A."

"What?" Deena said, reeling back.

"Hollywood," he said, his voice growing even more confident. "Listen baby, music is in my blood, but you are a product, and a truly successful product doesn't limit itself to one genre. I want to see you on more than just the stage. Your beautiful face was made to be larger than life—on the movie screen."

"Movie screen?" Deena said, still slightly confused.

"I'm starting a movie division within Rainbow

JAMES
HUNDER
EARLY

MEET
DREAMS
IT'S TIME · MOVE · DREAMGIRLS
I'M GOING TO THE FINISH LINE

Records," he said. "I've already hired this Hollywood producer, Adam Brooks, to run it, and he's already identified some fantastic vehicles for you. He's out in L.A. reviewing movie scripts as we speak."

"Wait, this is a done deal?" she asked.

"We move to L.A. in a month."

"What about our wedding? I never dreamed of getting married anywhere but back home . . ."

"You'll have the wedding of your dreams, I promise you. I'll buy you a mansion bigger than any home you could have ever imagined, and I'll fill it with beautiful things—your favorite things. You can plan your wedding in the garden, filled with all your favorite flowers. I'll hire servants who will cater to your every fantasy—your every whim. And I'll fly all of Detroit to California to witness me saying 'I do' to the woman of my dreams. It will be unforgettable—you'll see."

It was unforgettable indeed; Curtis made sure of that. He had the wedding, a fabulous affair replete with three thousand white roses, fifty doves, two live bands, reporters from *Ebony* and *Jet*, and four hundred guests including family, friends, and, of course, every celebrity you could think of witnessing the nuptials in the gardens of their sumptuous Beverly Hills estate, professionally produced—not just for their own edification, mind you, but for publicity purposes that had nothing to do with their expressing their love for each other. The wedding video was actually shot for a promo film Curtis was making to drum up excitement for Deena's film debut. It was Brooks's idea. He thought that if studio heads and film producers had a reel showing the Dreams' ascent from the rugged streets of Detroit to international celebrity, they would be more apt to envision Deena as a leading lady—specifically, the leading lady of the new film about Cleopatra.

Deena wasn't so sure the reel—or any of Curtis's fast talking, even—could make her capable of tackling a film role. She sat in the screening room in the basement of their mansion, watching nervously as a narrator strung together the story of the Dreams, beginning with an early photograph of Deena, Effie, and Lorrell that had been altered to replace Effie with Michelle. Deena winced and took another pull on her cigarette.

"It all started on the streets of Detroit, where three girls named Deena, Lorrell, and Michelle dreamed about one day becoming singing stars," the narrator started, as a clip from a network variety special showed Deena and the Dreams recreating their ghetto roots on a cardboard inner city set. They were wearing Afro wigs and tattered jeans, set off by inch-long eyelashes and rhinestone belts. "During their triumphant rise to international stardom, they've played everywhere, from the White House to Buckingham Palace," the narrator continued, the Dreams' song "I'm Somebody," playing softly under his voice.

Deena, taking her eyes off the screen only long enough to light another cigarette, watched nervously as the film chronicled their wedding and Curtis's stable of recording stars. She smiled at a still of Teddy Campbell, the ten-year-old singing and dancing lead of the Campbell Connection, and then sat up and listened intently as Curtis's face filled the screen.

"I think the reason our music is so popular is that it crosses all boundaries," Curtis said into the camera. "Pro-war and antiwar, young and old, black and white—everybody can relate to the Rainbow sound."

Deena smiled as she thought about Curtis's words, but then dropped her jaw when the narrator moved on to talk about what was next for the "king and queen of the music scene." "Deena Jones has conquered the worlds of music, stage, and television, and soon she hopes to take on her biggest challenge yet: movies," the narrator said, as a series of costume sketches depicting Deena as Cleopatra filled the screen. "Hollywood screenwriters are currently working on the epic, untold story of Cleopatra's early years, all set to the music of today."

Deena shot out of her seat. "Have mercy," she said, smooshing her cigarette into her crystal ashtray and rushing out of the screening room and down the hallway of her immaculate, well-appointed home. The sound of her high heels hitting the marble echoed against the walls; her bodyguard, Big Rob, followed at a discreet distance. "Rob, have the driver pull the limo around—I have to go to Rainbow Records immediately," she said.

"Is Curtis in his office?" Deena asked the receptionist before she even got to the doorway.

"Actually, he's in the conference room with Mr. Brooks, Wayne, C.C., and a few others. They're meeting about the Cleopatra film—congratulations!" the receptionist said warmly.

Deena didn't respond—she just walked past her as if she had neither seen nor heard what she said. "I'll wait," she said simply as she stepped through the door and into Curtis's inner sanctum. She closed the door behind her, and was immediately swallowed by the grand black-and-white image of her stretched across the length of the wall behind Curtis's desk. She stood there, staring at it, wondering how she was ever going to live up to the image her husband had created for her.

She wasn't the only one who had her doubts about Deena Jones, movie star. Turns out that in the conference room, Curtis was getting that news firsthand.

"Now I saved the bad news for last, Curtis," Brooks said, taking a big swallow before he finished what he had to say. The roomful of executives, including Wayne, C.C., and the cadre of white boys Curtis had added to the distribution, marketing, and promotions divisions of Rainbow Records, let out a nervous chuckle. "Paramount passed on *Cleo.*"

"Why?" Curtis asked.

"Too period. And they're not convinced Deena's got the chops," Brooks said simply, figuring it was best to just say it, rather than drag it out.

Curtis started working his jaw—a sign that he was pissed. When that happened, it was never good. Never. Everyone in the room looked down, steeling themselves for the wrath. "Do the thing, kid," Curtis seethed.

"Sorry, boss?" Brooks said, this time the only one chuckling.

"You know. The thing," Curtis said, tossing his hand for emphasis.

Brooks turned beet red, then slowly stood from

his cushioned chair. And then he started hopping on one foot and making ape noises, an act of punishment Curtis made him perform when he was in a particularly foul mood. The first time Curtis requested Brooks do this, the white boy refused—he wasn't about to denigrate himself like that in front of any man, let alone a black man. But he'd quickly hopped, if you will, into action when Curtis threatened to "toss him out on his monkey ass" if he didn't—an option Brooks, who had been fired from his last job as the head of a small studio because of slumping numbers and a nasty coke habit, could not afford. So he found himself hopping and making ape noises whenever Curtis was pissed, which seemed to be more often than not, these days.

Curtis laughed when he saw Brooks take flight. Everyone else eventually joined in on the joke—everyone, that was, except C.C. and Wayne, who looked at each other and shook their heads.

"Forget it. We'll finance the movie ourselves," Curtis said, slicing through the laughter. Brooks stopped jumping. The room was silent again.

Benita, Curtis's secretary, walked into the room, leaned down, and whispered in Curtis's ear; he stood abruptly. "Gentlemen? Meeting adjourned," he said, and walked out, Wayne and C.C. following close behind them.

"I just don't know how we're gonna swing that," Wayne said. "You're spreading yourself too thin as it is. The music side is starting to suffer."

"Music runs itself," Curtis huffed.

"Those days are over, Curtis," C.C. interjected. "Just putting Deena's name on a record doesn't make it a hit anymore. And our acts are dying on the road, especially Jimmy. He needs new material."

"Jimmy needs to sober up," Curtis said, stopping by his secretary's desk. "Wayne, start pitching the networks on an anniversary special. We'll put out a greatest hits tie-in, and it'll rake in enough green to make ten movies—and still pay for all you useless wannabes too."

Curtis left Wayne and C.C. standing there with their mouths agape, and rushed into his office. There he found Deena standing in front of the photograph, dwarfed by her own image. Curtis grabbed her from behind. "How's my favorite wife?"

Deena pulled away, nervous about what she was about to say, but resolved to say it. "Curtis." She hesitated. "I'm not sure how to tell you this."

"Just say it, baby," Curtis said, loosening his grip on her waist.

"I know how much time you've invested in this movie, but . . . I can't play that part," she said finally.

"Of course you can. You're just nervous, that's all—"

"No, Curtis, you don't understand," Deena said, cutting her husband off. "I don't want to."

Curtis took Deena's hand and led her over to the expansive couch lining the wall in a seating area overlooking the rest of his office. They both sat. "I promised I'd make you a movie star, and *Cleo* is gonna get us there. She was a queen, Deena, the ruler of a nation. Not some hooker/junkie/maid like the rest of the roles they have out there for black actresses."

"Oh, I know, Curtis, it's an important story . . ."

"And it's more than you. Just think about all those beautiful black women who ain't even been born yet. One day, they're going to say, I can play any part I want to. Look at Deena Jones, she did it."

"But it's ridiculous," Deena said, still unswayed. "She's sixteen years old for most of the movie."

"You'll always be sixteen to me," Curtis said, kissing her hand.

"Maybe that's the problem," she said, standing up and walking toward her picture on the wall. "Maybe you just don't see me for who I am."

"I know exactly who you are," Curtis said, walking over to put his hands around her waist again. "You're innocent and joyous and seductive and carefree and angry and full of attitude. And you're beautiful—the woman I've always dreamed of having by my side," he whispered directly into her ear. "Who would believe that the world would believe in my dreams? You are my dream, Deena; nothing will ever change that. All I want to do is make you happy," he said, turning her around. He lifted her face to his and kissed her lips ever so softly; she melted in his arms. "Tell me what I can do to make you happy, Deena."

Deena pulled back from his kiss, drunk from his passion. "You know what I want," she said.

"There's plenty of time for that," Curtis said, pulling back.

"Please Curtis," Deena implored. "Let me have your child."

Curtis started working that jaw again. "I have to get to another meeting," he said simply, and walked out.

"Magic, read your book," Effie snapped at the seven-year-old, a pretty, skinny little thing with her daddy's eyes and her mama's attitude.

Honestly, Magic had long grown tired of sitting in the corner of the cramped welfare office, listening to babies wail and watching those babies' mamas scowl as they huffed and puffed through their wait time for the next caseworker to dig through their personal business and admonish them like little children. And for what? A book of food stamps that was hardly enough to get them through a couple of shopping trips down to that funky, dirty grocery store over on Thirteenth Street, where they seemed to specialize in brown meat, half sour milk, dusty bags of beans nobody liked, and fruit that was more rotten than not. It hardly seemed worth it, even to this seven-year-old, who, because of her circumstances and mother, was much wiser than her seven years. Magic hated the welfare office and everything in it, and she couldn't understand why her mother put herself through the caseworker's nasty inquiries for such meager means.

Effie did it because she had no other choice. After Curtis kicked her out of the Dreams, she struggled to keep up her singing career, taking some of the songs C.C. had written for her and making a go of it as a solo artist on the chitlin' circuit. But she blew through half a million dollars in a little under two years trying to keep up the lifestyle she'd become accustomed when she was a third of a chart topping, internationally successful singing group. She didn't realize how much Curtis and Rainbow Records spent to finance their lavish lifestyle; all she knew was that Curtis and Wayne paid the tab whenever they left a hotel or a restaurant, their clothes were waiting for them when they hit the dressing room for their shows, and their airline tickets, hotel bills, and car services were taken care of before they stepped foot onto a jet, a car, or in a fancy establishment. If the girls needed money, they simply called Rhonda, who handled Rainbow Records' finances, and, almost as quickly as they'd ask, the girls would have a check waiting for them.

Within two years, after paying the whopping hospital bill for when she gave birth, and buying a house, and shopping for fancy clothes to perform in and financially supporting the pianist and bass player in her band, Effie's bank account was bone dry. And she could barely make any money singing because her weight made it all-too-difficult to make it to gigs. Those she did get to, she could barely sing through a set, what with the smoke and cramped quarters affecting her breathing and her vocals. No matter that she was a former singer in the Dreams, bar owners and patrons alike weren't checking for a has-been singer with a weak instrument. When her pianist left to play for a young local group with nary a hit to its name, Effie knew it was over.

By the time Magic had her third birthday, Effie had sold her house to pay down debt she'd wracked up on credit cards, and moved into a welfare hotel not too far from the projects where she grew up. Effie was a good mom—kept her daughter clothed and fed as best she could—but mostly, she found her joy at the bottom of a bottle of Southern Comfort and a good plate of neck-bones, white navy beans, and cornbread.

"I'm done," Magic told her mother, patting the cover of the book, which sat on her lap.

"Then read it again," Effie said, tossing a frown in her daughter's direction before she turned back to the case worker, a stocky white man with a receding hairline and wrinkles that seemed to stretch from his forehead to his jowl.

"Did you look for work this week, Miss White?" the caseworker asked, tapping his pencil on a pile of paperwork that cluttered his desk.

Effie rolled her eyes, sat back in her chair, and folded her arms. "Mister, you can keep asking me that question but the answer's always gonna be the same. The only thing I know how to do is sing, and since there ain't nobody lettin' me do that no more—no, I did not look for a job."

"Have you considered asking the girl's father for help?" the caseworker asked, looking down and scribbling something onto the paperwork.

"Magic don't have a father," Effie seethed. "Now are you going to give me my check or do I have to speak to your supervisor?"

The caseworker sighed, scribbled some more onto the paperwork, and then reached into his file cabinet, where he kept Effie's check in a folder marked with her name. "Here you go," he said.

Effie snatched the envelope from his hand and pushed herself out of her chair. "Come on here, Magic, let's go. If we hustle, we can catch the number forty-two bus back home," she said, looking from the clock to her daughter. "Come on now—get your book and let's go."

Effie and Magic made it to the bus stop in time enough to catch the 3:15 stop just a few blocks away from the welfare office. Effie crowded onto the vehicle, and signaled Magic to take a seat next to an elderly man who'd spread out his bags on the seat next to him, leaving little room for a grown person—much less a big woman like Effie—to sit. "There," Effie said, pointing, as she grabbed the strap to hang on. A young mother holding a small baby and a diaper bag in her arms struggled to squeeze past Effie, but there was no room for her to move. Magic turned away, embarrassed to see her mother, who by now was rotund and sloppy, blocking nearly the entire bus aisle with her body fat. Effie saw the look in her daughter's eyes, and felt her heart sink—again. She looked at her baby, and then beyond her, out the window and over Woodward Avenue, which was now a bombed-out wasteland—the remnants of the awful riots still searing its mark on what used to be the bustling, thriving heart of the colored community. No one had bothered to try to clean it up—white folks didn't see a need to, and black folks couldn't get it together enough to do it, either. And so the neighborhood just crumbled into a shell of its former self, much like the people—all too poor and too tired and too powerless to make it better.

"Are you ever going to work again?" Magic asked her mother, every bit as forthright as Effie.

Effie didn't answer. She was gazing out at Curtis's old dealership, where half the letters were missing from the "Sound of Tomorrow" sign, the windows were boarded up, and the building was pockmarked with grime and graffiti. Whenever she passed by, she bristled as if someone were boxing her ears, a feeling that made her heart race. She wanted to sit down, but there was so much more to do: Stop by the check-cashing place, then run over to the supermarket for those little groceries she needed, and maybe buy a toy or two for Magic, so she'd have something under the tree come Christmas Day. "You get off at the next stop and go straight up to the house," Effie told Magic, ignoring her daughter's query. "Your grandfather will be there waiting for you. I got a few stops to make."

By the time Effie made it up the three flights of

stairs to her apartment, the only thing she had on her mind was her bottle and her TV set. She said a silent prayer that her daughter was asleep when she finally pushed the key into her front door and walked in. Magic was asleep on the sofa, her face lit by a tabletop Christmas tree. Her father, Ronald, who'd come over to babysit while Effie shopped, was sitting at the plastic kitchen table, holding up a card. "It's from your brother," he said, smiling.

"Send it back," Effie said, dropping the groceries on the kitchen counter.

"There's cash in here," Ronald said.

"You spend it."

"Effie White, you are a mule," her father said, disgusted by the fact that no matter how hard he tried, no matter what he said, he couldn't get his daughter to let go of her venom toward Curtis and forgive her brother. Ronald had acknowledged often that C.C. could have handled the situation better, but he'd also assured her that she played her part in the whole mess, too. He'd done everything but pay his daughter to try to convince her to move on—to stop settling for government assistance and go out and do what she needed to do to use the fine instrument God had given her, a gift indeed. But Effie simply wouldn't hear of it, even when her father got so incensed he got to yelling at her, which, of late, had become about as often as Effie was liquored up. That was often.

Effie, not ready for another knock-down, drag-out with her father, headed over to the sofa and stroked her daughter's face. "C'mon, baby. Time to go to bed," she said to Magic, kissing her awake.

"Just as stubborn as your mother," Ronald continued.

"Go home, old man," she said, waving off Ronald as she lifted Magic and walked to her room. She stayed there until she heard her father quietly close the front door behind him, then headed into the kitchen and reached into the cabinet for her liquor bottle. She hesitated for a moment, and then slowly closed the cabinet door, leaving the bottle in its place. A commercial announcing a Christmas special for Rainbow Records blared from her set like a trumpet in her ear; Effie sat on the couch and stared at the screen. The Dreams were smiling, singing "Winter Wonderland," and then the group's theme song, "Dreamgirls," played under the announcer's words. Effie closed her eyes and listened for her voice.

Her eyes were still closed long after the commercial went off, long after whatever show was playing went off, too. She didn't hear any of it—just her father's words: "You're a mule," rewinding again and again in her mind. In a rare moment of clarity, Effie listened, and came to the only decision that made sense: She was going to Marty's office in the morning to get back what was hers—her career. Not just for her sake—but for the sake of her child.

SEVEN

No matter what he did, Jimmy just couldn't get his right leg to stop jumping. It was like it was up on stage already, dancing a jig, making his bell-bottomed pants flap against the stale, smoky air that filled Curtis and Deena's den. Even though his song, "Patience," was playing on Curtis's stereo, he could hear music playing softly off in the living room, Donny Hathaway's "This Christmas." Yeah, Donny Hathaway, smoothed out, Jimmy thought. But couldn't nothing top Hathaway's "The Ghetto," man—them bongos banging and Donny on the organ and the mic, riffing. Yeah, that was all the way live, Jimmy thought. That, and James Brown telling everybody to *Say it loud—I'm black and I'm proud!* Even Aretha was in on it, man—come on, *Think what you tryin' to do to me/Freedom! Freedom! Freedom!* All the true soul artists were using their music to give life to the movement—standing up in solidarity with the people in the streets, who were taking their water-hose beat-downs and police-dog growls and crooked-cop baton licks like warriors. Like men. Not that shuckin' and jivin' crap Curtis was shoveling onto the charts. Jimmy was a half a millisecond from slapping his hand over his mouth, he wanted so badly to say that out loud, but even in his manic state, he knew not to pick a fight with Curtis. Not when he was trying to convince his manager through song that it was time to take Jimmy Early and the Rainbow Records sound in a new direction.

"Patience little sisters/Patience little brothers/Until that morning of a brighter day," Lorrell and Jimmy's voices intertwined over the soaring ballad. C.C. nodded his head and mouthed the words as he reached over and began holding hands with Michelle, who recently had revealed she was sweet on her producer; Lorrell gently placed one of her hands on Jimmy's leg, and used the other to rub his back, hoping she could calm her boyfriend, who was fidgeting and biting his fingernails. *"Hey, hey, patience, patience/'til that brighter day,"* the record ended.

There was a long moment of silence as Jimmy, Lorrell, C.C., Michelle, and Deena held their collective breath, waiting to hear what Curtis, who'd listened to practically the entire song with his eyes closed, had to say. Finally, Curtis spoke. "It's good, man," he said. "It's really good."

Jimmy adjusted his rhinestone-adorned denim jacket, scooted up to the edge of the sofa, and broke out into a toothy grin, his sheer giddiness surpassed only by that of C.C., who practically had been holding his breath through the entire recording. He, too, was as nervous as—if not more so than—Jimmy, because getting Curtis on board with Jimmy's new single meant C.C. would have a good shot at altering the Rainbow Records sound to mirror what was going on with soul music and black artists who, more than ever, were standing in solidarity with the black power and civil rights movements. "We thought it'd be better to surprise you, Curtis," C.C. said, excited. "That's why we went ahead and recorded it first."

"Sort of like a Christmas present," Lorrell chimed in, smiling.

"And C.C.'s got the whole number staged," Michelle added, proudly patting C.C.'s hand.

Deena reached across to C.C. and touched his hand, too. "It's so powerful," she said. "I loved it."

"I tell you, Curtis," Jimmy interjected. "It's exactly what I need right now. Like you always say, brother. A new sound."

"Still, it's a message song," Curtis deadpanned.

The buzz in the room came to a halt—everyone stopped moving, and every smile that was on every face dropped.

"It tells the truth," said Michelle, the only person in the room who didn't have enough clear-eyed sense yet to know Curtis wouldn't give two humps about her convictions. "I'm angry. My brother's over in Vietnam fighting a pointless war, and I'm angry about it."

Inspired by his girlfriend—and perhaps a bit fearful that she was about to catch it, C.C. added his two cents. "That's right, Curtis. Isn't music supposed to express what people are feeling?"

"No," Curtis said, standing up. "It's supposed to sell. Trust me, Jimmy, we'll figure out some new material for you. Come on Deena, there's a guy I want you to meet," he said, walking to the door without so much as another thought, let alone another word, about Jimmy's song. Deena, embarrassed, stood at her husband's command. "Oh, and lose the shirt, blood. It's hurting your image."

Deena watched her husband leave the room, and then walked over to Jimmy, who, defeated, sank down into the couch. His leg was still dancing. "I'm sorry, Jimmy," Deena said, touching his shoulder. To the others, she repeated her apology.

No one acknowledged her words, or looked

at her as she slunk out the door. In fact, no one moved, except for Jimmy, who pulled a ball of tinfoil out of the front pocket of his jacket and cleared a spot on the cocktail table.

"Aw, honey, you don't need to be doin' that stuff right now," Lorrell said, frowning and shaking her head.

Oh, but Jimmy did need it. He did.

And he began to take it like people take their coffee in the morning, and their sandwiches for lunch, and their greasy chicken at suppertime—a little coke or speed to get up, some pills to come down, a little weed to clear his head, a little liquor to get loose. Drugs, he thought, were his salvation, the one lovely lady he could count on. Yeah, Lorrell was helping him out; she'd convinced C.C. to cut "Patience" for him, and when she was in town, she always gave a brother what he needed. But even that was becoming all too rare; she was always off somewhere, smelling Curtis and Deena's behind and riding around in her fancy cars and spending up that money—oh, so much money!—and singing on stages only white folks could really get comfortable on. And all the while she was off enjoying the accoutrements of a pop (read: white) star, Jimmy was feeling the pressure of an ever-shrinking fan base that was too preoccupied with The Dream and the war and real soul music to care about a slick, greasy Negro singing the same ol' do-wop-meets-rock-'n'-roll songs he was pushing seven or eight years ago, before Vietnam, before Malcolm and Martin got taken out, before everybody was taking it to the streets. His gigs were coming few and far between, and when he did have one, it was usually part of some ol' crappy soul music retrospective with a bunch of other washed-up artists whose records were collecting dust in America's basements.

Which left Jimmy to sulk at home with his old lady, Melba, a stern churchwoman who believed in the Lord and spending up all the money Jimmy made singing music she didn't listen to. Gospels, that's what she was into—that and her Bible and the pastor of Beulah Land Missionary Baptist Church and spending money on expensive cars, diamonds, and clothes. She didn't even bother to let him know when she was leaving the house—would just walk the hell out, and show up hours later with shopping bags in one hand, her Bible in the other.

Which was fine by Jimmy, because when Melba left the house, he could make love to his main lady, who asked for nothing but to be adored like a lover. And oh, Jimmy loved his white woman—his cocaine.

That fact was not lost on Curtis.

* * *

"Look man, let me rap with you for a minute," Curtis said, closing his office door behind Jimmy, whom he'd called in for a meeting at Rainbow Records.

"Sorry I'm late man," Jimmy said, sniffling and shaking that leg, his white woman practically rubbing a hot hole in his pants pocket. He wanted to get back home and strip naked and cuddle with her on the sofa in front of the stereo—caress her while he listened to a little Marvin Gaye. But Jimmy knew this was an important meeting; C.C. had already hipped him about a major TV show Curtis had planned for the Rainbow Records acts, and he had been waiting for the call to tell him he'd be performing. "I got caught up with some things, you know how it is. But I'm here, jack. What you got, baby?"

"Look here," Curtis said. "Dick Clark is hosting a special show featuring all the Rainbow Records acts . . ."

"Yeah, I heard a little somethin' about that," Jimmy said, rubbing his nose and trying his darnedest to keep that leg from jumping. "I'll be glad to do what I do, but you need to let C.C. work on some new material for a brother, 'cause—"

"Look here, Jimmy, let me lay this on you, brother," Curtis said, cutting Jimmy off. "I wasn't going to put you on the show, but the producers said they really wanted you on, because it would only be right to have my first act on a tribute show to me. So right now, I don't really have a choice but to let you perform. But let me tell you this one thing," Curtis continued, straightening up in his seat and leaning across his desk, "you gonna have to clean up your act, and you're going to have to do it now."

"Hold up—what you mean, man?" Jimmy asked indignantly.

"I mean you gonna have to stop messing around with them drugs and get right before you get out onto that stage. You have a problem, man, and we been friends for a long time now—done some dirt together, too, ain't we? Ain't we?" Curtis asked, waiting for Jimmy to answer him back.

"Sure, yeah—good times, man," Jimmy stammered.

"Now when I was first starting out in this business, you gave a brother a shot at the big time, and now I'm returning the favor by letting you onto this tribute show. If you cut out all that drugging and drinking, and get this show right, we can head back into the studio to see what we can do about that new sound you been talking about," Curtis said.

"But . . ." Jimmy started.

Curtis didn't really want to hear anything else from Jimmy, though. He'd long ago written Jimmy off—decided that he was never going to reach the heights Deena could because he wasn't capable of turning off all that street in him. He could give Jimmy Sinatra's "My Way," and Jimmy would pimp it so hard, not even Sinatra himself would recognize his own song. That just wasn't the sound Rainbow Records was striving for—and its impeccable image of wholesome, solidly upper-middle-class, apolitical black Americans certainly had no room for a boisterous, dashiki- and applejack-wearing, washed-up drug addict, as far as Curtis was concerned. But if Dick Clark wanted Jimmy on the tribute show, Curtis had to deliver, and so he would.

Curtis quickly stood up from his desk and extended his hand to Jimmy. "I gotta run, brother," he said. "Got a couple of meetings I got to tend to, you know how it is."

Jimmy slowly rose from his chair, his eyes red from anger. "Yeah man, go handle *your* business," he said. "I'm sure gonna handle mine."

"You do that, brother. You do that," Curtis said, moving toward the door. "Showtime is next Tuesday. My secretary will call you with the details. You'll be singing 'I Meant You No Harm,' you know, nice and low key. That's what they like, man, and it's already staged out so you don't have to worry about putting in too much practice."

"Yeah," Jimmy said. "Low key."

"All right baby, stay up," Curtis said, and walked out of the room.

Jimmy wanted to take his hand and sweep everything off Curtis's desk—pull the bookshelves down, break something. How, after all, did Curtis figure he was doing *him* a favor? *I put his ass on—if it wasn't for me, he'd still be selling broke-down Cadillacs on broke-down Woodward Avenue to a bunch of broke Negroes,* Jimmy thought. And now, here Curtis was, walking around acting like he was saving Jimmy—like he had to prove himself to get the star treatment to which he was entitled.

Jimmy knew better than to bust up Curtis's office, but he wasn't about to walk out of it without some kind of justice. So he pulled his white lady out of his pocket and used one of Curtis's business cards to spread her out in two straight lines on top of Curtis's desk. And then he sucked her like a vacuum cleaner, right up his pronounced nostril. "Yeah, I got low-key for you, all right," he said, licking his finger, wiping up traces of the powder off Curtis's desk, and rubbing it on his teeth. He spun around on his heels and clapped his hands, then practically skipped out of Curtis's office, down the steps, out of the Rainbow Records offices, and onto the street. He pulled the brim of his applejack down onto his brow to shield his sensitive eyes from the bright sun. He needed to get to a phone and talk to Sweets—Jimmy needed some candy. Enough to get him through to next Tuesday.

"Mr. Early, you're up next," the producer said, pounding on the door to Jimmy's dressing room.

Jimmy let out a grunt.

"I thought you were going to stay clean tonight, baby," Lorrell said as she tried to force Jimmy to drink a cup of lukewarm coffee. "You know how important this is."

Jimmy let out a sigh. "I was doin' just fine, honey, and then Melba started in on me. 'You never take me anywhere, Jimmy! I'm sick of staying home every night!'" he whined. "And then before I know it, she's coming down the stairs in her party dress!"

Lorrell reeled back. "Wait . . . wait a minute. Are you telling me your wife is out there? Right now?" she demanded.

"What could I do, baby?" Jimmy shrugged. "That's why I needed to relax."

Lorrell put down the coffee and reached for the champagne. "Here, sugar. Have a drink."

"Oh, thanks, Lorrell," Jimmy said, downing the drink.

"You know," Lorrell added sweetly, "it's our anniversary too, baby. Don't you remember? Let me give you a kiss for each year. One, two, three, four, five, six, seven, eight. Eight years of unmarried life."

"Oh don't tell me we're gonna start again," Jimmy huffed.

Just then, the stagehand popped his head into the dressing room. "You're up, Mr. Early."

Jimmy jumped up out of his chair and headed for the door.

"Don't you walk out on me, Jimmy Early!" Lorrell demanded as she chased Jimmy down the hall.

"I promise, Lorrell, I'll tell her," he said over his shoulder.

"But when, Jimmy? When?" Lorrell said, following him into the wings.

". . . Please baby, just a little more time."

"Time's run out, Jimmy. I get it now—I really do. You never really loved me," she said, shouting over the din of applause that accompanied Teddy and the Campbell brothers as they made their way off the stage.

"I love you, Lorrell. You know I do," Jimmy said.

Lorrell looked up at the love of her life—desperate to believe him.

"But right now, I got a show to do," Jimmy said.

Lorrell's expression hardened. "No more," she thought to herself. "No more."

Jimmy stepped onto the stage and dazzled the audience. *"And though it's hard for me to show it/I've got to let you know it/'Cause darling, I love you more each day/But the words got in my way/Oh I meant you no harm,"* he sang, his eyes settling on his wife, who was sitting in the second row. Melba nodded along to the lyrics, sure her husband was singing to her. But then Jimmy executed a smooth toe-cross-slide combination, and caught sight of Lorrell standing in the wings. He moved toward her and sang directly into her eyes. *"And I would die/If you ever said goodbye/I love you, I love you . . ."*

He swayed and turned back to the audience, focusing again on his wife, and then sang some more. And then his white woman decided it was time to sing a little ditty in her honor. Jimmy stepped forward and waved for the band to stop.

"I can't do it. I can't sing no more sad songs. Curtis, my man, this is your night, and there's got to be some good times!" Jimmy shouted into the mike. The audience laughed and applauded; Curtis waved at Jimmy, playing along for the cameras. Jimmy turned to the bandleader. "Brian, look, baby, I'm gonna give you a count-off. And the rest of you guys, you come in when I tell you, okay? One two, three—hit me! Bass man, come on up."

The bass began to bump.

"One, two, three—hit me!" Jimmy shouted. "Sound good. Saxophone—on the floor!"

The saxophone blew a mean note, falling right into stride with the funky base. Jimmy could see the cameras struggling to keep up with him as he moved across the stage. In the control room, the technical director frantically checked his cue sheet. "What's he doing?" he called out, but no one answered, so busy were they trying to catch Jimmy in his moment.

"One, two, three—hit it! Yeah! C'mon horns—hit it!" Jimmy screamed. The trumpets joined in. Jimmy launched into a gospel-tinged rap number:

Hey Curley
Let's rap with Jimmy Early
Got a home in the hills
Mercedes Benz
Hot swimming pool
Got lots of friends
Got clothes by the acre
Credit to spare

I could wake up tomorrow
And find nobody there
But Jimmy want more/Jimmy want more
Jimmy want more/Jimmy want more/Listen!

The audience went wild, clapping and bouncing in their seats as Jimmy pulled off his coat and tossed it away. He skipped across the stage, just like in the old days—drinking in every scream, every hoot and holler as he executed combinations he hadn't done in years.

Jimmy want a rib
Jimmy want a steak
Jimmy want a piece of your chocolate cake
But more than all that
Jimmy wants a break
'Cause Jimmy got soul/Jimmy got soul
Jimmy got/Jimmy got/ Jimmy got soul!

He ripped off his tie, then tugged at his shirt. C.C., who was sitting below in the front orchestra section, shook his head and laughed. Curtis tossed him a glare, then stood from his seat, a forced smile on his lips, and slipped out of the box. He rushed across the empty lobby and into a side door that led to the wings. He stood next to Lorrell, who was standing there shaking her head.

"Did you know he was going to do this?" he asked her.

"Curtis, I'm just as shocked as you are. We didn't see this in rehearsals."

"No kidding, Lorrell," Curtis said, his temple working overtime.

I can't do rock
I can't do roll
What I can do, baby, is show my soul

Jimmy turned and unfastened the top button of his trousers and loosened his shirt, yelling, "Jimmy got soul!" into the mike as the audience cheered him on.

Sooner or later/The time comes around
For a man to be a man
Take back his sound
I gotta do somethin'/to shake things up
I like Johnny Mathis/but I can't do that stuff
'cause Jimmy got soul, Jimmy got soul . . .

Jimmy turned around and pulled out his shirt-tails, and, when he did, his pants dropped to his ankles. The audience whooped—Melba let out a gasp and covered her mouth with her gloved, bejeweled hand. The technical director yelled into his headset, "Take it out!"

Almost immediately, each of the monitors cut away to a "Please stand by" card, so the audience at home didn't catch Jimmy doing his exaggerated double-take, pulling up his pants and taking his bows. He bowed one more time, blew a kiss to the audience, and then to Lorrell and Curtis in the wings, and hopped offstage.

"Hey Curtis," he said with a huge grin rimming his face. "You like my show?"

"You made a fool of yourself," Curtis said through clenched teeth.

"Now wait a minute—I was just being Jimmy," he laughed. Jimmy darted onstage and took another bow—the audience still clapping wildly. And then he scooted back to Curtis and Lorrell. "Lorrell, tell the man if you can," Jimmy said smugly, his eyes never leaving Curtis's.

Lorrell sucked in her breath and let her words tumble one over the other. "Jimmy keeps beggin' you for something new, but the way you ignore him makes him insecure. Of course, he's confused. It don't take a whiz to know that only a desperate man would drop his pants—in living color on network television!" Lorrell gushed, wheeling around to face Jimmy.

"Thank you, Lorrell. You told it like it is," Jimmy said, satisfied.

"Yeah, that ain't all I got to say to you, honey," Lorrell said, putting her hand on her hip. "You—"

Curtis cut her off. "Brother, my man—we're through," he said simply.

"Whatcha mean—whatcha mean we're through," Jimmy said, getting in Curtis's face.

"I'm sorry, Jimmy. Your time has passed."

"I got soul, man. You can't kill a man with soul," Jimmy said, raising his voice. By now, a producer with a clipboard was pacing nervously nearby, yelling into his headset. Deena and Michelle were standing nearby, a team of stylists and hair and makeup artists sending up clouds of powder and hairspray into the air and fussing with their outfits. Their band was setting up on the instruments Jimmy's band had just finished playing. The show was about to go on.

"Come on, let's try to end as friends. If you ever need help, just give me a call," Curtis said, extending his hand to Jimmy. But Jimmy didn't take it—looked at it like he would rather spit on it than shake it, then swatted it away. Curtis tossed him a glare, and walked away.

"Don't you worry, Curtis, 'cause I don't crawl. I'm an original! I don't beg," Jimmy called out after him.

Lorrell headed for the stage, where Michelle was waiting. But Jimmy caught her arm before she got too far away. "Wait a minute, baby, I need you now," he pleaded. "Baby, I love you."

Lorrell stepped up to Jimmy and gave him a deep kiss. "And Lorrell loves Jimmy," she said, looking into his eyes. "But Lorrell and Jimmy are through. I got a show to do, remember? I got a show to do," she said, pulling away as Melba entered backstage from the auditorium. She stared at Melba, who was staring back; neither said a word.

"And now, please welcome the brightest star in the Rainbow constellation—Deena Jones, with the incredible Dreams!" the announcer said over the speakers. Lorrell stepped onto the stage; Melba stormed out. Jimmy stood there, alone, watching Deena blow kisses at the audience, which was standing and cheering as she walked up to the microphone and threw a kiss to Curtis, who was taking his seat in the box.

Jimmy heard the white woman—his drug—calling him from his dressing room, and his leg started dancing that jig as soon as her voice reached Jimmy's ears. He scratched his neck and turned around to run to her, but he ran smack into a security guard as big as a wall.

"Time to go, Mr. Early," he said, putting his hand on Jimmy's shoulder.

Jimmy didn't move. "I don't beg, Curtis!" he yelled out, trying desperately to hear himself over the music and the roar of the audience. "I don't crawl! 'Cause I was here long before you and I'll be here long after y'all."

But no one heard him, save the security guard, who took him by the arm and helped him leave the pavilion—his white woman calling after him.

EIGHT

Even though she had on sunglasses, Deena still kept her head down as she moved through the hotel and toward the pool, where the film producer Jerry Harris and the director, Sam Walsh, were lounging in a cabana, waiting for her.

"You are an incredibly beautiful woman," Harris gushed as Deena settled into a chair opposite him. Deena's bodyguard stood watch near the pool, his hands cupped together and dangling in front of his black-suited frame.

"Well thank you, Jerry," Deena said, sipping her tea and flashing her signature demure smile. She wasn't quite sure what to make of Walsh, whose hippie attire and long, stringy gray hair, was quite the opposite of the look she expected from a powerful Hollywood producer. But Deena wasn't about to let him catch her off guard: She was on a mission to snatch one of the leads in *Vegas Score,* a movie she'd read about in the *Hollywood Reporter*. "Written and directed by Sam Walsh, and produced by Jerry Harris, the script is said to be a hot one," the story said. "Inside sources are already speculating that with the right casting, and Walsh in the director's seat, *Vegas Score* could easily be an Oscar favorite."

The role was exactly what Deena had been hoping for—exactly the kind of movie she wanted to, had to, be in. Curtis, you see, was still pushing that same tired ol' Cleopatra role on her, and, the way things were looking, she was going to be kicking forty by the time Curtis got the script together and the right producers to film. She'd said to him over and over that he should forget placing her in the title role, that she was much too mature for it. "Let Bebe Vine star in it, or Debbie Bulloch," she'd told Curtis, offering up two younger singers from the Rainbow Records label for the part. But Curtis wouldn't hear of it.

"It's being written specifically for you, and there's no way we're going to rip it up now—I've invested too much money in it for that," he'd said. "Let me just handle the business, baby, and you keep doing what you do best. Don't worry your pretty little head about it anymore."

Well, Deena had stopped worrying about it

long ago and decided to take matters into her own hands. She'd grown tired of being the quiet, shy puppet of Curtis Taylor, Jr., and knew enough about the business, and specifically about her husband and the way that he did business, to recognize that everyone in the Rainbow Records stable was expendable. Even Deena Jones. She had, after all, had a front-row seat to the ever-unfolding drama played out as Curtis unceremoniously slashed and burned through singers, songwriters, producers, bandleaders, secretaries, janitors—hell, anybody he figured wasn't fitting into his tight little pop music mold. She really didn't give a damn about the fate of a lot of them—that was the way careers went in the music business, no matter who's making the decisions. But when Deena witnessed Curtis systematically disassemble Jimmy Early's career—the man that had led them all down the road to stardom—she knew that she, too, could easily become dispensable. And she wasn't about to stand around and wait for it to happen to her, so Deena Jones decided that Deena Jones, *her* product, was going to go for hers. When she saw the item in the *Hollywood Reporter*, she had her assistant set up the meeting. "And um, keep this between you and me," Deena told her. "I want to surprise Curtis, okay?"

Jerry Harris shifted in his seat when Deena

smiled and thanked him for his compliment. "No, I mean—you're *too* beautiful," he said. "This movie's about three grifters heading to Vegas for one last score. When Dawn goes down on that truck driver, you have to smell her desperation. It's gotta be ugly. Raw."

Deena turned "it" on. "I know, that's what I love about her. There's no pretense, no fucking bullshit," she said, tossing in the curses for a little extra bite.

Harris turned to Walsh, shocked. "Wow! America's sweetheart has a potty mouth." Harris laughed.

Deena picked up her tea. "Of course if I were to become involved, we'd have to do some work on the part," she continued.

"What do you mean?" Walsh asked, sitting up in his seat. "I spent a year on this script."

"And it's good," Deena assured him. "But she's not real yet. To start with, what kind of name is Dawn? I've met a lot of sisters in my life, and not one of them was called Dawn," she added, tossing in a little black girl attitude for added effect. She knew she'd gained some ground with the neck roll.

"The script is a blueprint—nothing's written in stone," Harris said. "Isn't that right, Sam?"

"Maybe we can get together when Al's back

in town. Run through some scenes, play around with it?" Walsh said, addressing Harris more so than Deena.

"I'd like that," Deena smiled.

"I hear Curtis is still trying to get that crazy black 'Cleopatra' made," Harris said. "Christ, wasn't the Elizabeth Taylor version bad enough?" Walsh laughed nervously. "You know it'll ruin him. I've seen it happen over and over again, guys who spend ten bucks to make five. Is it true he's got mob money in this thing?"

Deena had anticipated this question, and had told herself she'd have to play it cool. "My husband has his hands full with the music side right now," she said simply. "That's why I didn't want to bother him with our meeting here today."

Everyone knew this was a lie, but, in true Hollywood style, they agreed to ignore it.

"But let's say we decide to get in bed with you on this. Will Curtis even let you do it? I hear you're on a pretty tight leash. A diamond collar, but a tight leash," Harris said.

Let her do it? See, this was exactly the crap Deena was talking about—Curtis had so much control over her that even men she'd never met before knew that Deena was powerless over her own schedule, her own body. *Her* product. Well not anymore.

"That won't be a problem, Jerry," Deena said, pursing her lips. She took another sip of her tea.

Deena was quite pleased with herself, so much so that later, in the studio, her sheer giddiness practically leaped from her lips as she wrapped her voice around a new song Curtis and C.C. had been working on. But even as she poured her happiness into the song, it was hard to ignore the raging argument playing out in the control booth, right before her very eyes. Michelle and Lorrell, who were rocking out to the thumping bass line of the soupy, synthesized track, sang their "ah, ah, ah, ahs" as they looked first at each other, their eyebrows furrowed, then back at the picture window that gave them a clear view of Curtis and C.C. going at it like they were about to tear each other apart. When C.C. got in Curtis's face, Deena snatched her headphones off, thinking she might have to go in there and remind them that they were in the middle of a recording session, not on some street corner. But then C.C. burst out of the studio, Curtis in hot pursuit.

"I didn't think it was possible, Curtis," C.C. yelled, as Michelle, Deena, and Lorrell rushed out of the studio to intervene. Deena's assistant, Esther, was already waiting in the hallway, but neither Curtis nor C.C. noticed her standing there. "I didn't think you could squeeze even more of the soul out of my music."

"I just made it more danceable," Curtis reasoned.

"What about the lyrics? That rhythm takes all the feeling out of the song," C.C. said.

Curtis, growing impatient, breathed a heavy sigh. "This is what you've been asking for—a totally new sound, bigger than rock or R&B ever was. People are getting ready to boogie again, and when they do, they'll be dancing to our music!"

"Your music, Curtis," C.C. practically spat at him. "It has nothing to do with me."

"Aw, come on, brother—you're my main man," Curtis said, reaching for C.C.'s arm. But C.C. brushed him off and rushed away toward the offices, where his briefcase and freedom awaited.

"Kiss my ass. Brother," C.C. yelled.

He stopped when he saw people emerging from the offices, gathering in the halls. Rhonda and Janice were crying; others were hugging. "Now what's going on?" Curtis asked, exasperated.

And then a sharp scream pierced the air, making nearly everyone who heard it jump, if even a little. It was Lorrell, hopping up and down in anguish, tears mingling with her black mascara, streaming down her face. Deena was trying to hold her, but Lorrell was lashing about, crying uncontrollably—inconsolable. Michelle slowly turned to C.C., and, with tears in her eyes, told her boyfriend the horrible news: Jimmy Early was dead.

News of Jimmy's death spread quickly enough for TV cameras to get to the scene, so the television reporters were all the more eager to lean into their microphones with the salacious details of the singer's demise as their news stations constantly ran clips of Jimmy's body, covered with a white sheet, being carried on a stretcher out of a seedy hotel in downtown L.A. "Police say that Mr. Early had been dead for over a day, the apparent victim of a heroin overdose," the reporter said into the camera. "Plans are being made to fly the body back to Detroit, where there will be a private burial."

C.C. and Michelle stared blankly at the television set that stood at attention on the floor of Curtis's den. Curtis, stricken with grief, downed a glass of Scotch to comfort himself. Over in his bedroom, Deena was trying her best to comfort Lorrell, who, after disappearing for several hours, had showed up at the Taylor residence in even more of a mess than she was at the studio when she'd first learned of her lover's death. "My God," Deena had said when she rounded the corner into the foyer and saw Lorrell slumped on the floor, her hair and clothes askew, her makeup running all over her face. "Somebody help me!"

Curtis stood by while C.C. and Michelle helped Deena get Lorrell up the spiral staircase and into the master bedroom. Lorrell couldn't even look at them, couldn't, until after a long time of silence passed, even speak. Her throat was sore from all the screaming she'd just done over at the hospital, where she'd had her driver rush her after she'd learned of Jimmy's death. "What do you mean I can't see him?" she said tearfully as the guard nervously shuffled papers on his desk. The morgue where Jimmy's body lay waiting to be officially identified was just behind him, beyond the swinging doors. "Jimmy and I, we were in love. Surely, it won't hurt you to let me see him—say goodbye. Mister, please . . ."

Just then, the doors swung open, and out walked a man in a white coat, followed by Melba, who, her head down, at first didn't see her husband's girlfriend standing in front of her. "Again," the coroner said, "I'm really sorry for your loss, Mrs. Early."

"Thank you . . ." Melba began, and then stopped when she realized Lorrell was standing before her. "What are you doing here?" She glared, her words punctuated with so much venom that spittle landed on both her and the coroner's face.

"I . . . I . . ."

"I, I hell," Melba seethed. "You have some nerve

showing up here, like any of this concerns you. Let me tell you something, little girl," she said, walking up and pointing her finger in Lorrell's face. "This here? This is my husband. Mine! Not yours."

"But all I did was love him," Lorrell said weakly. "I just want to say goodbye."

"Get. The. Hell. Out. Of. Here," Melba said, before spinning around to the coroner. "Do not let this woman anywhere near my husband's body, or I will press charges against her, you, and anybody else that has anything to do with this godforsaken place."

The words were still ringing in Lorrell's ears as she lay in Deena's arms, still unable to quite comprehend how she was going to go on without her beloved Jimmy. "She won't even let me see him, Deena," said Lorrell as Deena rocked her. "She won't let me see my Jimmy."

Out in the den, Curtis was shaking his head at the television. "What a thing. A bad, bad scene."

"Well . . . thanks for the drink," C.C. said, getting up to leave. He helped Michelle out of her chair, avoiding even looking at Curtis.

"Tell Lorrell I'll stop by tomorrow," Michelle said, grabbing hold of C.C.'s hand.

"C.C. . . . no matter what troubles we've had—there ain't nothing as important as family," Curtis said as C.C. walked toward the exit. C.C. stopped, but didn't turn around to face Curtis until he said the three words he'd waited all day to say.

"It's over, Curtis."

"Jimmy did this to himself," Curtis called out. "You know that."

C.C. had no more words. He simply grabbed Michelle's hand and walked on.

"Michelle," Curtis said sternly, stopping her in her tracks. "C.C. can quit. You can't."

C.C. tried to reconcile in his mind how Curtis could be so cold-blooded and calculating, even at a time like this—when they'd lost a brother, a man they loved like one. After he dropped Michelle off at his place, he drove straight to the airport and took the first flight to Detroit, where he drove around the streets of his hometown, recalling the days he ran them all, trying to get somebody—anybody—to listen to his music, hear his sister's voice. He passed Buddy's Corner Shop, where he and the girls sang their first song to a public audience—a bunch of drunks who waited outside the store's doors for enough spare change to put a little bottle or two in their wrinkled paper bags. Just a little farther down was the courtyard where he and Effie sat and watched the cars go by while they wrote his third song, "Moody Girl," in honor of the first girl to kiss him and then leave him for another boy. And then there was the Detroit Theatre, standing in the midst of it all, a broken-down shell of its former self—so full of memories. There was a time when he couldn't even imagine what it would be like to hear his songs on the radio, much less see them at the top of the *Billboard* charts, and now that the unfathomable had occurred, he couldn't quite see how it could all come to an end like this. Detroit was broken. The group was shattered. Jimmy was dead. How could Curtis be so low—make him so low. He'd given up everything to follow that man—his passion for soul music, his creativity. His family. He wanted so badly to be with his family; death does that to you—makes you want to grab hold of the people around you, and reach out to the ones who weren't there, to make amends. Effie was on his mind, and he needed to find her, to tell her that he wanted—needed—her forgiveness.

It was their father who let C.C. into his sister's apartment. He waited there for nearly two hours, all the while wondering how Effie could have spiraled into such squalor and degradation. "But I sent her money—didn't she get it?" he'd asked his dad.

"She got it."

"Well, wasn't she using it? I mean, I've sent her enough over the years for her to live better than this—to have a better life than this," C.C. said.

"She wouldn't spend it," his father said as he opened a drawer in the breakfront in Effie's tiny living room. He pulled out a box, opened it, and walked over to C.C. The box was full of letters—C.C.'s letters—most of them unopened, all of them full of the cash he'd sent her. "Your sister," Ronald said, "is a mule."

C.C. shook his head and walked around the tiny apartment—watched the roaches as they scurried along the near-empty cupboards, ran his fingers across the blankets piled neatly on the pull-out sofa in the living room, presumably where Effie slept, since there was but one bedroom, and it was filled with toys. A child's room. He was sitting on the child's bed when he heard Effie's voice calling out "Hey" to a neighbor; he ran to the door and opened it, peering over the stairwell to catch his sister and her young daughter coming up the stairs.

Magic took the steps two at a time. "What's a wake?" she asked.

"It's when friends get together and share their love for someone," Effie said as she struggled up the steps.

"Mama, why are you always so slow?"

" 'Cause I'm old, baby," Effie said simply, ignoring yet another insult from her daughter. She stopped to catch her breath while Magic ran to their apartment. She stopped short when she saw the strange man standing in the doorway.

"Who are you?" she asked.

Effie, seeing C.C., headed back down the stairs, her heart pounding with anger. C.C. headed down the stairs after her. Their father, Ronald, appeared in the door and took Magic by the hand. "Who is that man?" she asked.

"That's your uncle, little girl."

"Effie!" C.C. called out again. He heard the door slam a few flights down, and cursed under his breath. His sister was never one for making anything easy, but he knew this. He ran down the stairs and out into the darkness, but his sister had made herself invisible. If he looked just a little while longer, he would have seen her hiding herself and her tears in the shadows of the huge oak tree where Effie once sang one of C.C.'s songs so passionately that they both cried. She loved him—missed him some, too, but she knew she'd let the anger envelop her for much too long, and now she just wasn't quite sure how to pull herself out of it. *Daddy,* she thought, *is right. I am a mule.*

C.C. slowly dragged himself back upstairs to Effie's apartment to bid his father goodbye.

"Don't give up, son," Ronald said as he enclosed his son in his warm embrace. "She needs you now more than ever, even if she acts like she don't.

Find her, son, and make her understand that she's more than this."

This was what C.C. was thinking about as he bent himself over a club soda the next night at Max Washington's Club, where some Detroit musicians gathered to jam and trade stories about Jimmy. Effie was sitting at a front table with Marty, with whom she'd reconnected and started working with to secure some local gigs. C.C. sat at the bar, unsure how to approach them, knowing that whatever words came out of his mouth would never make up for the years of abuse he allowed Curtis to heap on the two. So he sat and drank and watched.

"You know, he wasn't 'Thunder' Early then, just Little Jimmy," a jazz singer said to Marty and Effie as she prepared to sing a tribute song to her old friend. "How old was that boy, Marty?"

"I don't know. Prob'ly twelve," Marty said.

"Well, he had the hands of a fella twice that age, and he wasn't shy about using them," the jazz singer laughed.

"Oh yeah, Jimmy was a real little shit," Marty said, nodding. "A real little shit." Marty started to tear up; Effie put her arm around him as the jazz singer nodded at the piano player. The melody was soft and mellow; the jazz singer's voice crackled above the notes, scratching out a love song for a friend gone on. *"I miss you, old friend/Can I hold you? And though it's been a long time, old friend/Do you mind?"* she sang.

Effie had made a vow not to drink again, and had promised Marty, too, that she would stay dry if he agreed to help her get her career back on track. Marty, now a graying old man with a lot of memories but little to show for them, wanted to get back in the game the right way, without the vices that stalled—and, in Jimmy's case, killed—careers, and so he made her promise to leave the liquor alone if they were to work together. Effie was determined to keep her vow, but it didn't help that she was sitting in the middle of a bar, depressed over the loss of her friend. "I'm going to get some club soda," she said, getting up from the table. "You want anything?"

"Nah, baby, I'm all right," Marty said.

Effie walked over to the bar and, out of the corner of her eye, she caught a glimpse of C.C. She had a feeling she would see him there—her father had told her as much—but still, she wasn't prepared to talk to him. In fact, she really didn't have anything to say to him, even after her father implored upon her to at least listen to what her brother had to say. "He's not working with Curtis anymore, Effie," Ronald told her when she finally did come back home after she first saw C.C. standing in her doorway. "He's going to be striking out on his own, and he wants to help get you a record deal."

"I don't need his ass," Effie insisted angrily. "I didn't need him then, and I don't need him now."

"Oh, but you do, sweetheart. Family needs family. This ain't got nothin' to do with money or singing or what happened in the past. This is your flesh and blood."

"Funny how he wasn't thinking about that when Curtis kicked me out my own group and—"

"Did you really expect your brother to give up on his dream, Effie? Would it have made you happier if he came home with you, and missed out on his blessings? All those years, he was doing what he'd dreamed of doing, writing hits—hearing his music sung all over the world. Are you that selfish that you wouldn't want that for your brother?"

Effie knew her father was right, but she still wasn't going to make it easy for C.C. to just walk back into her life.

"Effie," C.C. said, walking over to her as she waited for her drink.

"What gives you the nerve, C.C.? Coming here after all these years?" she burst out, angry.

"Effie, there's nothing I can say . . . except I was young and I made a mistake."

"I'm telling you, I won't be used. Not by you, not by anybody. Never again."

"I promised I'd write you a hit song, Effie. Let me do it for you now."

"I don't need you," she spat.

"No, Effie, I need you," C.C. said, moving closer to his sister. "It's been all these years, and you haven't even said hello. I'm your brother, Effie. Say hello. You know I'm sorry. I should have come before today."

"You've always been the baby," she said, fingering the rim of her glass.

"But I'm trying to change," C.C. said.

"And so am I," said Effie.

"It's taken all these years to be free," he said.

"You know, I loved Curtis for a long time after what happened," she said. "And it took a long time to get ahold of my anger. I thought it was all behind me, but when you came here, and with Jimmy dying, it all just came rushing back."

"It took me all these years to find myself, and realize that I have a song—a real song. And I think only you can sing it the way it should be sung. Effie, let me help you," C.C. said, putting his arm around his sister. "Let's do what we always wanted to do—together."

Effie didn't speak for a long while, just sipped her club soda. The two of them listened to the jazz singer riff through "My Funny Valentine," a song Effie used to sing, with her brother accompanying her on their beat-up, out-of-tune piano. Effie closed her eyes and listened to the woman bend and twist her pearly voice around the words. It was a lovely instrument, that woman's voice, but Effie imagined blowing a little more smoke into the bridge, and pulling hard on the words *stay, funny Valentine—stay* until the stretch moved the audience to its feet.

"I've waited so long to hear you say that to me," Effie finally said after she opened her eyes. "Say it again."

"Effie, sing my song the way it should be," C.C. said, leaning in to embrace his sister.

The two of them didn't waste any time getting into the studio. Marty made the arrangements, and C.C., still bringing in money from his songwriter and producer royalties, paid the bill. Effie did what she did best; she leaned into the microphone, and let loose a voice that was pure honey.

You want all my love and my devotion
You want my loving soul right on the line
I have no doubt that I could love you/forever
The only trouble is you really don't have the time
You've got one night only
One night only
That's all you have to spare

One night only
Let's not pretend to care
One night only
One night only
Come on, big baby, come on

C.C. was in the control booth, running the mixing board, taking in the sound of his music—his sister's music. The way he'd always imagined he would.

Magic sat next to the radio, listening intently to her mother's voice in the song. Effie, C.C., and Ronald watched her, almost as proud of the song as the little girl was proud of her mother. Magic snuck a look at Effie, trying to make the connection between the person she lived with and the voice she was hearing.

"And that was Detroit's own Effie White, formerly of the Dreams, with her new hit song, 'One Night Only.' I tell you, that Effie White is one bad mama—the great voice of the Great Lakes. You heard it first, right here!"

C.C., Effie, and Magic all clapped wildly as the deejay went to commercial.

While Effie and her family were busy celebrating her newfound success, Curtis was back at Rainbow Records in L.A., listening to a cassette of "One Night Only" that Wayne scored from Nicky Cassaro, who, under Curtis's direction, was tracking the song's success. His temple jumped—his eyes narrowed like slits as he turned off the player.

"He thinks he's making a fool of me," Curtis said to Wayne.

"Nicky says the record's only got local distribution, black stations mostly. But it's starting to take off."

"If C.C. wrote it, don't I own it?" Curtis said, leaning forward in his seat.

"Technically yes, at least until we settle his contract. I'll get the lawyers to draw up a letter and demand half the royalties."

"No. This is the perfect song to launch the new sound. I want to rerecord it with Deena and the girls."

Wayne wrinkled his brow; he knew that was some low-down stuff right there, and for perhaps the first time in his career as Curtis's flunky, he didn't hesitate saying it. "Come on, Curtis, their record's already moving."

"So what?" Curtis said dismissively. "If I can buy a hit, I can buy a flop."

"Hey man, this is Effie's big break. There are other songs," Wayne reasoned.

"This is business, Wayne. Now get on it."

It didn't take them long to get around to knocking off Effie's song. Curtis gave the cassette to his latest creation, a duo of songwriters out of Philly known as the Pulley Brothers, whom he'd hired to replace C.C. as the head of Rainbow Records' production staff. The brothers added lush strings under Deena's much more seductive vocals to change the song—make it more the pop feel Curtis was looking for to take his company's sound in a different direction.

"Okay, we're going to run through it right quick," Eddie Pulley said into the microphone from the control booth. "I'll play the music so you can get a taste of the beat, and then Raymond will work with you on the lyrics."

None of the women recognized the song; they hadn't heard Effie's version of "One Night Only."

Within a week, with Nicky's help, the song was ready for release, Detroit deejay Elvis Kelly was driving a shiny new Cadillac, and Deena Jones and the Dreams' hit record, "One Night Only," was playing on the radio. And when the group exploded onto the spotlight-covered stage at the massive New York Dance Club, Curtis was smiling down from his perch above the dance floor, a grin spreading across his face. He knew from the first note that he'd struck show business gold for the second time.

That was clear to Effie, C.C., Marty, and even Magic as they watched their worst nightmare unfold on Effie's TV screen. They'd heard the song on the radio, and for a minute, a few deejays were even playing the songs back-to-back, asking callers which version they liked best. But right there, on the Johnny Carson show, Curtis was winning the war, one note at a time. Again. Deena, looking ever glamorous in a striking, glittering, silver floor-length gown, burst ahead of Michelle and Lorrell, shook her shoulder-length wig, and sang the words—Effie's words.

Magic shot her mother a disappointed, almost angry look.

"I'm so sorry, Effie," C.C. said.

Effie squeezed his hand, a gesture that assured him she didn't blame him for what happened. Effie had been to the pits of hell chasing her dream, and had retreated into a hot hole in its bowels while Curtis dragged everything she'd worked so hard for away from her. This time, she was strong. Mad as hell, and strong. Because she knew that no matter what, everyone would see through this. They would see and know the kind of snake Curtis was. Effie watched as Magic moved to her bedroom, where her daughter buried her face in her pillow, and cried. She knew, just knew, that her dream of seeing her mom make it—get out of her long-held funk—was about to be realized. In her eyes, her mother was finally taking charge—finally doing something to change their lives, get them out of the ghetto. Be somebody. And now, it was all shattered. The strength she thought her mother had wasn't real. She was weak, Magic thought. Incapable of getting it right—and saving her from the misery, the only thing she'd ever known in her eight young years.

And while Magic's tears soaked her pillow, Deena was backstage in the NBC Studios, snatching off her wig. "Why didn't someone let me know he was going to ask me about Effie's song?" she demanded of her assistants and the publicist who'd accompanied them to *The Tonight Show.* No one answered her. "He might as well have accused us of stealing it!"

"That's what we did, isn't it?" Lorrell muttered.

"What did you say?" Deena said, reeling around to face her.

"I'm just saying, surely you couldn't have thought that no one would recognize the politics behind all of this. Effie's song was on the radio, we took it, rerecorded it, put our version on the radio, and crushed her. Again. Shoot, that's a TV show in and of itself—better than any soap opera my ass has ever seen!"

"Ladies, really, maybe we ought to wait until we get back to the studios to talk about this . . ." the publicist interjected.

"Get my things," Deena said, snatching her coat. "I'm ready to go. Now!"

TEN

The butler popped a bottle of champagne and filled Deena's glass as Curtis droned on some more about *Cleo* to his half-interested wife. This wasn't the role she wanted, and she couldn't quite find the right words to tell her husband that just earlier that day, after countless secret meetings and negotiations with Walsh and Wright, she'd finally signed the papers to play the lead role in *Vegas Score.* She knew he'd be pissed; Curtis had invested countless hours and as much energy into pulling his movie vision together, so much so that he'd almost let the music side flounder. He'd been banking on Rainbow Records' foray into disco to bankroll the project, with the hopes that it would be such a success he could put the money back into the recording side of the label, and then sign some new talent to revive the business as the landscape of the pop charts evolved into a jungle of glittery disco beats. Deena knew all this because she'd begun asking some questions of her own, been checking into some things to see exactly what her husband had planned for the business—for her. Just a few days earlier, she'd snuck into his office and nervously shuffled through paperwork on his desk and in his file cabinets. She wasn't quite sure what she was looking for, but she was tired of being in the dark—tired of feeling like she was property with no right to know what her next move was until Curtis told her what it was. She wanted information. She wanted more power. She wanted freedom. And she knew she could find it in her husband's office. Her fingers trembled as she fingered through the details of the plans Curtis had written up for the group's short tour to promote its new album. She was happy to discover that, beyond the tour, she was free. She also found out a few other surprising tidbits when she came across all manner of playbills, old pictures, ticket stubs, and notes and records of the beginnings of Rainbow Records, but nothing that would be relevant to their conversation now. She didn't, after all, want to talk about old times; she wanted to talk about moving forward. She was ready to let him know that she'd signed that contract—was trying to find the words to say to her husband, the man who'd guided her and told her what to do from the time she was but seventeen years old, that she'd made a decision about her career all on her own. Deena looked around her dining room—ran her eyes over the exquisitely carved dining table for twelve, and the elegant crystal service that cradled their roast duck and sweet potato purée, expertly fixed and served by their cooking staff. Her eyes settled on the portrait of her and Curtis that hung above the expansive cherrywood buffet; in it, Curtis was sitting in a Louis XIV armchair, Deena standing over him with her arms placed gently on his shoulders—he the kingmaker, she his faithful follower. Servant. Letting him know she cut the strings wasn't going to be easy.

". . . so Cecil Osborne finally committed," she heard Curtis say when she focused on his words. "He's soaking me for a million bucks but it's worth it, the man's great with actors. This is your first film and you're going to have the best, sweetheart . . ." The butler filled Curtis's glass and glided off. Deena fidgeted with her napkin. "What's wrong?"

"Nothing, Curtis. I guess I never really thought it was going to happen."

Curtis smiled. "You made it happen, baby," he said as he cut into his meat. "You're the queen of disco."

"Maybe I'm just tired . . ." Deena started.

"Of course you're tired, it's been a crazy time. Interviews, the photo shoot for *Vogue.* And all those meetings by the pool."

Deena looked up, shocked. *How on earth did he find out?* she wanted to say out loud.

"Do you think I'm stupid?" Curtis asked, coolly lifting his glass to his lips and raising his eyebrows. He took a sip. "When were you going to tell me?"

"I'm sorry, Curtis, I should have talked to you. It's just . . . it's such a great part, and exactly the kind of movie I should be making." Now Curtis was silent. "Nobody knows music the way you do, Curtis," Deena rushed, trying to sugarcoat her words in hopes her husband, who was visibly upset, would calm himself. "The music business is in your blood. But movies are different."

"Do you know why I chose you to sing lead, Deena?" Curtis asked, dismissing his wife's words. "Because your voice has no personality. No depth. Just what I put in there." Deena's heart did a double beat as Curtis's words sank in. He'd intended them to hurt, and they did. "No one understands you the way I do."

Deena considered the implication of what he was saying: Her husband was telling her straight to her face that she didn't understand herself—

and that just wouldn't do. Now she was pissed. "They offered me the part and I'm taking it," she said simply.

"Oh yeah? Read your contract. Baby, you can't even take a shit unless I say it's okay," he said quietly.

"I'll get myself a lawyer," Deena said, conviction filling her voice, even if she wasn't as confident on the inside.

"What, you think those honkies are gonna sit around and wait while you take me to court? Forget it, Deena. It's over," Curtis said, pushing back his chair and standing. "I'm sorry, honey, but I won't let those men handle you. They don't know how. And don't worry, Deena. I forgive you."

Deena stared down at her plate in misery as he walked away. She heard him close the door to his office, a sound that snapped her to attention. And just as simple as that, she knew what she had to do.

"But I don't understand why you need to do it this way," Deena's mother pleaded with her daughter, who'd called her mom from her private line in her dressing room.

"Mama, if you don't understand by now, you never will," Deena said simply. "This man will ruin me if I don't move right now."

"But you could ruin everything that you two have built together. It's just as much your record company empire as it is his," May insisted. "I just don't see why the two of you can't come to some kind of agreement . . ."

"Curtis doesn't agree with anybody who doesn't agree with Curtis," Deena snapped.

"But you're his wife . . ."

"I'm his employee—he said as much when we were sitting at that table," Deena said softly, trying hard to get her mother to understand. "I have to do this, Mama—there's no other way."

"Just think about what you're doing," May said.

"I have, Mama, now I've got to go," Deena said, before hanging up. By now, hot tears were dropping from her eyes onto an old, crinkled piece of paper she'd kept in her jewelry box, beneath the necklace compartment. On it was Effie's address and phone number. Deena scribbled the address across a yellow envelope, then stuffed it with paperwork and sealed it shut. She wiped more tears from her eyes as she put on her raincoat and snapped its buttons as she walked to the kitchen to summon her driver. She would have asked Benton to take the envelope full of Curtis's personal papers to the post office drop herself, but she had the sneaking suspicion that it was he who'd told Curtis about her meetings at Paramount. This mission she'd have to complete on her own.

* * *

Effie immediately recognized the handwriting, and cocked an eyebrow when she saw Deena's name scribbled at the top of the envelope. "After all these years . . ." she said as she turned it around and around in her hands. She was tempted to take a lighter to it, so uninterested was she in what Deena had to say, even if it was a pages-long heartfelt letter. But it was just that which piqued Effie's curiosity: What was it that Deena had stuffed into that big ol' envelope?

Effie struggled back up the staircase and walked into her apartment, where she and C.C. had been working on a new song. "You ain't gonna believe what I got here," Effie said, ripping the envelope open. C.C. let his fingers linger on the piano keys, looking up only after Effie shoved the envelope in his face. In her other hand, she held a handwritten letter, which she was busy reading, and a bunch of tattered yellowed papers.

"Dear Effie, here's your ticket to stardom. Deena," the letter read simply.

Effie quickly scanned the papers, not quite understanding what she was looking at until she got to a few pages with charts full of deejay names, radio stations, addresses, and what appeared to be money amounts. At the top, someone had scrawled, "Curtis, these stations have been taken care of. Have C.C. drop off another package, and I'll get to the next ones on the list." It was signed, "Nicky."

"C.C., your name is on here," Effie said. "I don't understand what this is," she said, leaning over her brother and shoving the papers in his face. "Who is Nicky?"

C.C. stopped playing and focused on the papers. When he realized what he was looking at—a list of deejays who'd taken payola in return for pushing Rainbow Records up the Top 100 chart—he snatched them from Effie's hands and quickly flipped through them all, taking in every word. He grinned first, and then laughed out loud. "Hot damn, ol' girl finally got her a spine, huh?"

"What, C.C.?" Effie said, smiling, but not quite sure why. "What are you talking about?"

"This here is our ticket to the stage, big sis," C.C. said, standing up from the piano stool. He planted a sloppy wet kiss on Effie's cheek. "It's on now, baby."

The lawyer with whom C.C., Effie, and Marty met the very next day agreed. "Without question, this could bring down Rainbow Records," said David Bennett, the attorney the trio procured. "It's plain as day that Curtis Taylor and his honchos bought their way onto the radio stations and the pop records charts. The scope of this investigation could be monumental, with deejays and radio stations across America going down on federal racketeering charges. Payola is illegal, and if the charges prove true, Mr. Taylor will be in a lot of hot water."

"Hot damn," Effie said, clapping her hands together. "I don't know what he did to Deena, but she done cooked his goose good."

Marty put his hand on Effie's shoulder, signaling for her to calm down. "There's more, though," Marty said. "C.C.'s name is on those papers—he was a part of this. Is there any way to protect him?"

Bennett shuffled the papers and shifted in his chair. "Look, Mr. White, I can't lie to you: If this goes to trial, you're going to go down with this thing. Your name is mentioned several times in the most damning files."

C.C. hung his head. Just a few nights before, Marty and he had discussed the implications of going to the law with charges that Curtis had cooked his books to make Rainbow Records one of the top labels in the world, and it was clear that if Curtis went down, C.C. would, too. At first, it didn't matter to him, so ready was he to bring Curtis down. But it was Effie who'd begged him to let it go—to spare himself the repercussions of being intricately involved in Curtis's payola scheme. "I won't have my little brother going to jail for that bastard," Effie practically spat once Marty and C.C. made clear that taking Curtis down meant C.C. could go down, too. "He's done enough to this family—I won't let him take you away from me again."

"But don't you see, Effie? This is precisely why I need to do this," C.C. said softly, walking over to Effie and putting his hands on her shoulders. "I'm your brother. I was supposed to protect you, but instead, I let that guy hype me up and believe that all of this—paying off the deejays, kicking you out of the group, all of that was what I had to do to make it to the top. But I'm through rolling over for Curtis Taylor, Effie. I'm through. And if paying for my actions is the only way I can make him pay, then that's the way it's going to go down."

"Hold on, there, youngblood," Marty chimed in. "I don't think Curtis is going to man up and go to jail over this. I got the feeling he's going to do exactly what we want to save his ass. Don't you worry about it—let me handle this, okay?" Marty said, embracing Effie and C.C.

"Mr. Bennett," Marty said, sitting forward in his chair in front of the lawyer's desk, clearing his throat. "I have a proposition for you: If you take on this case, and help us convince Mr. Taylor that he would be best served if he agreed to the conditions of a little business venture Mr. White and Ms. White here have in mind, we're prepared to make you a very generous offer."

"Go on," Bennett said.

"Well, it's like this: Mr. White here is an internationally known songwriter who, until this time, has worked with some of the most successful groups in the world."

"Yes, I know," Bennett said, smiling. "I'm a big fan of Deena Jones and the Dreams, the Campbell Connection, Jimmy Early. Shame what happened to him."

A vision of Jimmy's funeral flashed in Marty's mind; his bottom lip began to tremble, but he quickly got ahold of himself. "Look, we're going to be setting up a new record label under Mr. White's auspices, but we need help convincing Rainbow Records to release him from his contract," Marty said. "If you help us in this regard, we'd like to hire your firm to represent the interests of the company, a deal that I'm sure your superiors will remember come time to pick a new partner, huh?"

Bennett thought about the implications of what Marty was saying. He'd been working at Whitestone, Berger, English for five years, and had a roster of impressive clients, but none with the star power like that which came with C.C.'s name.

Bennett recognized that he couldn't lose—if he helped with the case, he'd be the brilliant lawyer who brought down one of the most well-known, well-respected record labels in the business. If he helped Marty pull off his plan to help C.C. start his own label, Whitestone, Berger, English would become Whitestone, Berger, English, and Bennett. "You've got a deal—we'll leave for L.A., um, how does next Tuesday work for you all?" he said, flipping through his appointment book.

"Next Tuesday will be just fine," Marty said. "Just fine."

The lights were lowered, but still, Deena had her eyes closed. She needed to see the words in her mind's eye, feel them in her soul. She pushed them out with an intensity Curtis had never heard before.

Listen to the sound from deep within
It's only beginning to find release
The time has come
For my Dreams to be heard
They will not be pushed aside and turned
Into your own all 'cause you won't listen
Listen, I am alone at a crossroads
I'm not at home in my own home
And I've tried and tried to say what's on my mind

You should have known, oh now I'm done believing you
You don't know what I'm feeling
I'm more than what you made of me
I followed the voice you gave to me
But now I've got to find my own

Deena's voice soared above the music—boomed when she sang, *I'm moving on,* just the way they had when she'd been practicing the words earlier in the studio by herself. She read them, each and every one, her eyes poring over the letters, taking in the true meaning of what she was about to sing. It was almost as if the writer knew what she'd done—knew she'd betrayed the man she'd loved a lifetime, who created her from the Detroit dust. But she had to stand up now, get off Curtis's back and walk on her own two feet. Finally, Deena felt like Effie and Lorrell had so long ago—like a grown woman. And the richness of that feeling, the boldness of it all, came out in every single note that passed her ruby lips, and filled her heart with emotions she could barely contain—sadness, elation, excitement, fear.

Curtis was mesmerized listening to her bend and curve the notes, moved. He decided right then that he would save the take, stash it in the vault for some use much later, and make her do another, more clear, more pop version of the piece, which the Evers Brothers had given him just the day before. Curtis adjusted the mix buttons on the board and sat back to take in more of Deena's performance just as Wayne stepped into the control room. He leaned into Curtis and whispered, "C.C. and Marty are here with some white man, and they're asking to see you."

"Well just tell them to go away," Curtis said, muting Deena.

"I'm not sure that's a good idea," Wayne said.

"What you mean, man? I'm working here. Tell them to make an appointment with the secretary or something."

"Actually, Curtis, I think you really need to go in there and see about this. They say they've got some papers with Nicky Cassaro's name all over them."

Curtis stood up in exasperation and headed out of the control room, without so much as a word to Deena, who stopped singing when she saw her husband rush out.

C.C., Marty, and Bennett were sitting in the conference room talking quietly when Curtis breezed in. "Well, Marty, it's been a long time."

"Yeah Curtis, and you're still a second-class snake," Marty said, unable to control his anger, despite that Bennett had warned them to keep their cool and let him handle the conversation.

Curtis sat down and put his feet up on a nearby chair. "Gentlemen, please. Give me a break," he said.

"Why, Curtis, did you give Effie one? I could kill you for what you did to her," C.C. spat.

"I assume there's a reason you all barged in here. Other than insulting me, I mean?" Curtis asked.

Bennett sat up in his seat and took over. "Mr. Taylor, we're planning to go to the federal authorities," he said.

"Who's this cat?"

"I'm David Bennett."

"Our lawyer," C.C. said.

"Yeah, we're going to tell the feds how you killed Effie's record. Payola, man."

Curtis listened with a patient smile, unmoved.

"Remember, Curtis, I've witnessed it all. The whole dirty operation, going back to 'Steppin' to the Bad Side.' "

"You're talking through your hat, baby," Curtis said coolly, his eyes narrowing into slits. "And who's gonna listen to you anyway? Just another guy who's pissed off 'cause he got fired."

Bennett opened his briefcase and started placing copies of the paperwork Deena had sent on the conference table. "We have documented evidence, Mr. Taylor," Bennett said smugly. "Falsified sales orders to cheat investors out of their profits. Good-quality merchandise listed as cut-outs to disguise the fraud."

Curtis and Wayne exchanged looks as Bennett kept pulling papers out of his bag.

"Mob-backed loans. And a payola operation stretching back eleven years."

Curtis picked up the papers and glanced at them, instantly recognizing them from his private files. "Who gave you these?"

"You're going to jail, mister," C.C. said.

"Yeah, well, I won't be the only one," Curtis said, his anger starting to show.

"You don't understand, Curtis," C.C. seethed. "I don't mind going to jail if it means they put you away for a long time."

Curtis flipped through the documents, getting more agitated. "How did you . . . these are private papers. No one has access to them except me and my—"

A look of dread crossed his face as he started to piece together how Marty and C.C. got hold of the paperwork. Deena had betrayed him. *But when, and how did she know what to look for?* he thought.

As Curtis listened to and pondered the plan Marty and C.C. laid out for him, Effie was in the studio with Deena. She burst into laughter. "Don't you wish you could see his face right about now?"

Deena smiled, but she wasn't happy—by any

stretch. It wasn't easy for her to send those papers to Effie, and it certainly wasn't easy for her to lounge around her house, pretending all was well between her and Curtis—not when she couldn't even stand to feel so much as his feet touch her while they lay in bed together. She had been anxious, wanted to know what Effie was going to do with the information she'd sent her, and what Curtis would do once he found out Effie had it. How her life—her career—would change.

And now she was standing in front of Effie, silently praying that what she'd done to her husband could help make up for all the dirt she'd inadvertently helped Curtis do to a woman who had been there for her, even when she was a bony, wide-eyed bookworm with little more than the ability to hold a backup note behind her friends.

She reached for Effie's hand. "How many times I wanted to see you, Effie. I kept wondering, Is she all right? Are you all right?"

"I'm happy now, Deena," Effie said. "I have a child who loves me."

"You have a baby?" Deena asked, happily surprised.

"Well, Magic's not exactly a baby anymore. She's almost nine now."

Effie's words hit her like a body blow. She did the

math, and knew instantly that the one thing she'd wanted all her life, the one thing that Curtis refused to give her, her husband had given to Effie.

"I wanted to tell you. At the time, I really wanted to tell you," Effie said, lowering her eyes. Just then, the door swung open and Curtis walked in. "Deena, he doesn't know," Effie said quickly to her friend, whose eyes were fire red with anger and grief.

"Well, Effie, I see you're just as much trouble as you ever were," Curtis said, walking up on the two in the lobby.

"Hello, Curtis. You haven't changed much, either," Effie shot back, giving him the once-over. "Actually, I take it back. You're looking a little heavy, baby. You could lose some weight," she added as she stepped out of the room.

Curtis followed her out, but first he turned to Deena. "I'll deal with you later," he seethed.

Effie walked out to the lobby, where C.C., Marty, and Bennett were waiting for her. Curtis followed close behind. "So?" she said, smiling.

"Mr. Taylor agrees that it's in everyone's interest to resolve the situation without resorting to draconian legal measures," Bennett said.

"Say that in English," Effie said, twisting her lips on the side of her face.

"Nationwide distribution for our version of

'One Night Only,' Effie," C.C. said, a grin spreading across his face.

"On our own label," Marty added.

"And all of it paid for by Mr. Taylor himself," Bennett said.

"Hmm. Sounds good to me," Effie said, laughing.

"And remember, Curtis. If these negotiations fall apart, you're going straight to jail," C.C. said.

"That's right, Curtis. You stopped me once, but you're never gonna stop me again. 'Cause this time, Effie White's gonna win," Effie said, turning on her heels and bopping out the door, Marty, C.C., and Bennett following behind her.

Curtis didn't bother watching them walk away—he wanted too badly to get back to the studio to talk to Deena. He burst through the door, yelling her name before his toe even hit the threshold. But the room was empty—Deena was gone. Curtis sat in the chair and buried his face in his hands, and started to run a reel of memories through his mind—of starting the label in his car dealership, banging out songs into the middle of the night with C.C., for the love of music, touring the chitlin' circuit, riding on that funky bus, playing cards and drinking and laughing with the band until they curled up in those rickety seats and caught a little shut-eye. Curtis had taken all of them out of the projects of Detroit and made them stars—made people all across the world know their names and crave their music. "This—this is the thanks I get," Curtis said out loud. "This is the thanks."

ELEVEN

A taxicab was waiting in the circular driveway when Curtis pulled up in front of the house he shared with his wife. He snatched the keys from the ignition, jumped out of his car, and took the front steps two-by-two. Curtis blasted through the doorway and rushed into the foyer. "Deena! Get your ass out here!" he yelled up the spiral staircase. He swung around when he caught sight of someone walking out of the den out of the corner of his eye. It was Deena's mother, who, unbeknownst to Curtis, had flown in from Detroit four days earlier. Deena had set her up at the Beverly Hills Hotel, where the two of them were taking meetings with record company executives who were clamoring to sign her to a solo contract, and real estate agents who were desperate to get the commission that would come with finding Deena a mansion worthy of an international pop sensation. "I must say, I'm surprised you're leaving Rainbow Records," the executives said repeatedly as they signed confidentiality agreements Deena had her lawyer draw up for the occasion (she still wasn't sure who told Curtis about the *Vegas Score* meetings, but she had a sneaking suspicion that her bodyguard and driver were handing over to Curtis a daily itinerary of her whereabouts, and filling in the details of what she was doing in her meetings when she had them).

Certainly, Deena was capable of handling all the proceedings on her own; she wasn't a stupid girl, and whatever she didn't understand, she had her lawyer explain in detail. But she needed the support of someone she could trust who wasn't on her or Curtis's payroll, and right then, at that very moment, the only person who fit the bill was May, her mother.

"Hello, Curtis," May said, crossing her arms.

"May, what are you doing here?" Curtis asked, forcing a polite smile to his face. "I thought you hated L.A."

"Oh, I do," May said. "But my daughter said she needed me, and so I'm here."

Just then, Deena came down the hall. "Go wait in the car, Mama," she said, swinging past Curtis as May shot one last look at her son-in-law and made her way to the door.

Curtis waited for the door to close behind May before he spoke. "Baby, that was a real nasty trick you pulled on me," he spewed.

"I had to do something to stop you," Deena said, still moving. "How could you do that to Effie?"

"I did what I had to do," Curtis said, following behind her. She walked into the den, where a suitcase lay open on Curtis's chair. "Where do you think you're going?"

"Out looking for a new sound, baby. Just like you."

"Come on, Deena. You can't leave."

"Why?" she yelled. "Because you own me? You can sue me, Curtis, you can take everything I have. But it doesn't matter, 'cause I'll start over. Effie did it, and so can I."

"I'm not living without you, Deena."

Deena folded her suitcase closed, willing her tears not to fall. Curtis put his arms around her, confident that with just a little pleading, he'd convince his wife to stay. "I love you, baby. You're all I can see," he said, watching with satisfaction as Deena closed her eyes. "You are my dream."

"But now I've got dreams of my own," Deena said, slowly lifting her face to her husband's. "And I can't let you take my dream from me. I won't. And I can't stay here anymore. I'm sorry, Curtis," Deena said, lifting her suitcase. "Goodbye."

Curtis stood by helplessly in the driveway, his empty, glittering mansion glaring over his shoulder like a scratched, dull diamond, and watched as Deena and May sped away. "To the airport, please."

Deena was still quite anxious when the airplane landed in Detroit, but the moment she got into her mother's car, rolled down the window, and breathed in the air, she felt a calm wash over her. The closer they got to her mother's house, a grand affair situated not too far from the Michigan River, the clearer she was about what she had to do: She needed to call Effie and C.C., and get them on board with her plan.

"Do you really think after all these years that Effie will want to sing with you again?" May asked as she and her daughter sat down to the smothered pork chop and dirty rice dinner she'd prepared.

"I don't know, Mama," Deena said. "I can't say I blame her if she says no. But I have to ask her if she'll be a part of the Dreams' farewell tour. It will be spectacular, the three of us back up there on the stage, together again. Plus, I owe her that much, don't I? We can both say goodbye to the Dreams, and hello to a new beginning."

"Well, I hope she can see that blessing through the haze of hate she's held for you and Curtis all these years," May said, cutting into her pork chop. "She'd be a bigger woman than me."

"Trust me, Mama, if I can meet Effie on her own terms, which I'm prepared to do, she'll run with it," Deena said. "She'll do it."

And Deena was right, but she had to do more than meet Effie halfway. Indeed, she had to go back to the 'hood, meet with Effie at her rundown apartment off Woodward Avenue, a street on which she hadn't been in years. Deena climbed out of her mother's car and looked up at the hotel where Effie was living, ran her eyes over the buildings connected to it—which had long been disconnected from her world. She shook her head. "Come on, Mama," she said, walking toward the entrance.

When Deena knocked on the metal door of Effie's third-floor apartment, C.C. opened it, and greeted her with a tremendously welcoming hug. "Come on in here, girl—everybody's been waiting for you," he said as he grabbed her hand and walked her into the apartment. Lorrell, Michelle, and Marty were seated at the tiny kitchen table; Effie was on the sofa, stroking the hair of her daughter, who was curled up next to her.

"Hey everybody," Deena said weakly, for the first time unsure whether she'd be able to do what she was so confident about on the car ride over. The quick once-over she gave the apartment made her stomach queasy; she couldn't believe Effie was living like that.

"Hey," said everyone, except Effie.

"Have a seat," Effie said, patting the tattered sofa.

"Look, let me just get to it," Deena said. "As you probably know by now, and for reasons you're all aware of, I've left Rainbow Records. I'm going to be getting my own solo deal."

"I figured as much," Lorrell said, sitting back in her chair. Lorrell had used the last week to think about her life, and how much she'd enjoyed stardom, but also how much she'd missed. She'd spent all that time doing shows, recording, doing press, making sure that she was properly coiffed even if she stepped out to the grocery store—but for what? Sure, the money was good, but she had nothing to show for it—not really. She'd told anyone who would listen that when Jimmy died, a little piece of her went right into that coffin with him. But Lorrell knew a huge part of her life had ended way before Jimmy took his fatal dose of drugs—ended the moment she agreed to play house on the road with a man who didn't belong to her. *"Wasted years,"* she sang around her house, a sad ditty she wrote in her head as she twirled around in her mind what she was going to do with herself. Going solo wasn't an option. Getting a life—a quiet one—she decided, after about a week of deep deliberation, was. "I can't say I blame you, what with all that's happened," Lorrell said to Deena. "To tell you the truth, I'm tired. I've been thinking about retiring anyway, getting me a little house somewhere, one of them big TVs, maybe a husband and a baby or two. We done missed out on a whole lot of living, ain't we?"

"We have," Deena said, looking at Magic. She touched her on her leg. "We sure have."

"You called this big meeting to tell everybody they don't have jobs anymore?" Effie asked, unmoved.

"No, not at all, Effie," Deena said. "Actually, I came here to ask if you'd be willing to work with me again."

"Work? With you?" Effie asked incredulously. "Seems to me the last time we tried that, it didn't work out too well."

"Hold on now, Effie, let the woman speak," C.C. said.

"Seems to me like you should be moving with a little bit more caution, too, C.C.," Effie shot back.

"Effie, I'm a businessman, and I'm a lover of music. Anybody who's got a plan for how I can do what I love is gonna have my attention."

"I think I already know this all too well," Effie replied.

"Look," Deena said, "I didn't come here to get anybody upset. I came here with a business proposition. I want us to have a farewell concert here, at the Detroit Theatre. Lorrell, Michelle, and I will perform . . ."

"What in the hell does this have to do with me?" Effie asked.

"It has everything to do with you, Effie," Deena said, turning to her. "Don't you see? When we get to our signature song, I want you to sing the lead, Effie, because you deserve to sing it."

Effie pondered the proposition, but wasn't yet convinced it was as good an idea as everyone else seemed to think it was. Getting up there on that stage would be too painful, she thought—bring back too many memories about her life lost. "I don't know about that," she said quietly.

"Effie, it will be a huge deal, and I'll make sure the audience is stacked with record executives and producers who will be begging to work with you after they hear your voice," Deena implored.

"And Curtis?" Effie asked.

"He has nothing to do with this, really he doesn't," Deena said. "And the contracts and stuff are for the lawyers to sort out. All I know is that we don't have to let that man ruin our dream again. Ever."

"Come on, Effie, how about it?" C.C. said.

"Yeah, come on, Effie," Lorrell said. "Let's do it."

Lorrell had the driver pause under the marquee at the Detroit Theatre, and smiled at what she saw. It read, "Deena Jones & the Dreams: The Farewell Performance."

"You never get used to seeing the Dreams in lights, right?" Deena said, leaning over Lorrell's shoulder to look at the marquee. "We should get inside," she added before nodding to the driver to pull back to the stage entrance.

Not an hour later, you could feel the electricity in the air, as a black-tie audience filed inside the theatre. Curtis stepped out of his limo, and was escorted by his publicist to the press line.

"This must be a bittersweet night, Mr. Taylor," one reporter said. "How's it feel to be saying goodbye to the Dreams?"

"They're all talented ladies and I respect their decision to explore new opportunities," he said. "Besides, I don't believe in goodbyes, just hellos. And I want you all to say hello to Tania Williams," he said, signaling to a beautiful girl who looked barely older than Deena was on the night she met Curtis. "We're releasing Tania's first album next month, and let me tell you, it's dynamite. A totally new sound."

Curtis was drowned out by fans who were screaming as Effie stepped onto the red carpet, with C.C. and Magic in tow. "Miss White," a reporter yelled to her as she stepped to the press line, not too far down from where Curtis was still being interviewed. "Your record's gone to number one. You must be pretty excited."

"It feels good, yes," Effie said.

"Any plans to move to California?"

"No, this is home," she said. "Besides, people are too skinny there."

The reporter laughed, then focused on Magic. "Who's the little lady, Effie?"

Effie glanced at Curtis, who was passing her as he headed toward the theatre. "This is Magic. She's my daughter," Effie said.

Curtis stopped and knew instantly that Magic was his. She was beautiful—indeed, she did have his eyes, and Effie's smile. He drank his daughter in; his heart swelled with pride. Curtis's eyes met Effie's; he continued into the theatre.

Inside, the announcer introduced the show. "Ladies and gentlemen, in their farewell performance—the incredible Dreams!" he shouted.

The audience stood on its feet and cheered wildly as the Dreams rose from the stage floor, wearing glamorous metallic gowns. Deena, Lorrell, and Michelle were frozen in place; Deena took a breath and waited for the cheering to stop. Deena winked at Lorrell and Michelle as they slowly turned to face the audience. They could see Marty, May, and Ronald down front; Michelle caught a glimpse of C.C. and blew him a kiss. Fans were already wiping away tears as Deena sang the first verse of their opening number.

We didn't make forever
We've each got to go our separate way
And now we're standing here helpless
Looking for something to say
We've been together a long time
We never thought it would end
We were always so close to each other
You were always my friend
And it's hard to say goodbye my love
It's hard to see you cry my love
Hard to open up that door
When you're not sure what you're going for
We didn't want this to happen
But we shoudn't feel sad
We've had a good life together
Just remember
Remember
All the times we had . . .

When they finished the song, the Dreams raised

their hands in a smooth, precisely choreographed wave, capturing their essence perfectly. The audience went wild, and kept up the energy all the way through the show, jumping to their feet, clapping and singing along to every word.

Finally, as the show wound down, Deena walked to the lip of the stage. "Well, I guess it's about that time. The last song. You know we've been together a very long time. I promised Lorrell I wouldn't cry," Deena said. Lorrell waved her away, her eyes brimming with tears. "And I'm not, I'm very happy. Because all of our family is here tonight. There aren't really three Dreams, you know—there are four. And we're really happy because tonight, we're all here to sing that song for you. Effie . . ."

The crowd practically lost its collective mind as Effie entered to the triumphant strains of "One Night Only." Deena, Lorrell, and Michelle touched fingers and stepped back as the song blended seamlessly into "Dreamgirls." She sang lead on the song, backed by the beautiful gospel harmony of the Dreams. When Effie's eyes connected with Magic's, her heart swelled—she could feel the pride her daughter had for her.

Finally, Effie had taken her rightful place.

And it was amazing.

Acknowledgments

All praises due to my God for opening doors and giving me the strength, courage, and wisdom to walk through them.

For my husband and long-time collaborator, Nick Chiles, and our beautiful daughters, Mari and Lila: Thank you for giving me the energy and passion to make it do what it do.

For my daddy, James Millner: Thank you for your steady, clear-eyed encouragement, even when I doubt; it is on your shoulders that I stand, and Mommy's memory that I move.

For my brother, Troy; my in-laws and best friends, Helen and Walter Chiles and Angelou and James Ezeilo; my spunky nephews, Miles and Cole; and all the rest of my beautiful and extended family by blood, relation, and friendship: Thank you for respecting—and encouraging—the hustle.

For my editor, Will Hinton; my agent extraordinaire, Victoria Sanders; and Amistad editor Dawn Davis for calling me off the beach and putting me to work on a fantastic, unforgettable, and historically important project.

And for Bill Condon and the cast of *Dreamgirls* for your passion and commitment to quality stories about the African American—indeed, human—experience.